Lolo Weaver
swims upstream

polly farquhar

HOLIDAY HOUSE · NEW YORK

Library of Congress Cataloging-in-Publication Data

Names: Farquhar, Polly, author.

Title: Lolo Weaver swims upstream / by Polly Farquhar.

Description: First edition. | New York : Holiday House, 2023. | Audience:
   Ages 8–12. | Audience: Grades 4–6. | Summary: Stuck in summer school and
   grieving over her grandfather's death, everything seems to be falling apart for Lolo
   Weaver, so she hatches a plan to fix things by stealing back her grandfather's dog,
   whose new owner happens to be a new classmate from summer school.

Identifiers: LCCN 2022021880 | ISBN 9780823452095 (hardcover)

Subjects: CYAC: Family life—Fiction. | Summer—Fiction | Schools—Fiction.
   Dogs—Fiction. | Pets—Fiction. | LCGFT: Novels.

Classification: LCC PZ7.1.F3676 Lo 2023 | DDC [Fic]—dc23

LC record available at https://lccn.loc.gov/2022021880

ISBN: 978-0-8234-5209-5 (hardcover)

For my sternman
(Unless you're the bowman? Either way, we paddle together.)

Chapter 1

My name is Lolo Weaver. It's a nickname. Lolo. The summer school teacher would only call me Willow, which is my official name and the one that gets printed up on the class lists, but when she was going around the room and my friend Eddie, whose given name is Eduardo, said, "Call me Eddie," she made a note in her grade book and always called him Eddie, even when she scolded him. When she got to me, the very last kid on the list, she called out, "Willow Weaver," and I said, "It's Lolo," and she said, "What kind of name is that?"

Every kid looked at me. Most of the kids were ones I'd known my whole life, and a few were from another school in the district, across the lake. The kids I'd known my whole life didn't know Lolo was a strange name. I didn't, either.

The teacher said, "That's like calling you Low-Low with a *W*." She lowered her voice when she said it. *Low-Low*. "It's a name with low expectations."

The teacher's name was Mrs. Cryer, and I thought maybe her name was exactly right since she'd make all her students cry because she was so mean. Not tough, but mean, because there's a difference. But I wasn't brave or stupid enough to say that, though I always wished I had. I might as well have, because I was going to get into other kinds of trouble that summer anyway.

Because it was summer, the building was mostly empty

and mostly quiet, but it still smelled like a school—like glue and pizza, and canned peas and dirty feet. The only difference was the hot summer sunshine that shone in, even when the blinds were closed, and how a person can't just sit inside a classroom without knowing that everyone else was on summer vacation. We were all there because we were the only ones who hadn't passed the state test.

At least the lake was closed, and at least that wasn't my fault.

***

Mrs. Cryer had excellent posture, the kind my gram was always nagging me about while poking at my shoulder blades, and even though she'd called my name, Weaver, which is always the last name on the list, she kept standing in front of her desk with her grade book and her teacher pen. It's the kind that has two ends, one blue and one red. That first day of summer school was the day I learned her name, but I already knew who she was, because Mrs. Cryer is Sycamore Lake famous. Every year, she is the Statue of Liberty in the Sycamore Lake Fourth of July Boat Parade. She stands tall and straight with her arm up in the air with a torch and wears a big, green pointy foam hat and gray robes. She stands out at the front of a big pontoon boat (my grandmother calls them party barges) and leads the parade.

I'm almost always the last name on the class list, so I was surprised when Mrs. Cryer didn't close up her grade book and get down to summer school business. She still had one name left. She was out of order, I guess, going back for a kid who hadn't answered.

"Noah Pham? Still no Noah Pham?"

No one answered.

Mrs. Cryer sighed. "Okay then." Just as she had raised her pen to cross the name off her list, the door banged open.

Even though I'd never seen him before, I knew the boy was Noah Pham, and Noah Pham made a big entrance. He was just late, but the way the door banged and the way he jumped into the room, as though he really was in a hurry to get to summer school and being late was like a fire in his pants, made it dramatic. If I were late, I'd try to sneak in. Turn the doorknob so slowly it hardly made a noise and then only open it wide enough to slide through and then slink over to the first empty seat. But not this kid.

He was from across the lake. That's why we didn't know him. There was another boy in the class, Max, who was also from across the lake, but it seemed that everybody knew him from soccer. Noah Pham was sweaty. His dark hair stuck up as though summer sweat was a hairstyling product. His glasses—the sturdy kind I bet his mom picked out from the display of glasses that were supposed to be unbreakable and had a replacement guarantee—slid down his nose. He was still catching his breath. He said he was sorry. His bus was late.

Mrs. Cryer nodded. She didn't have anything to say about that, which was lucky for this Noah Pham kid. She just stood as straight as the Statue of Liberty, holding her grade book closed and pointing, also like the Statue of Liberty, to an open seat by the windows.

Chapter 2

We started that first morning of summer school with brand-new composition notebooks that didn't lay flat yet—you had to bend them back if you wanted them to stay open—and brand-new pencils. Mrs. Cryer had gone around the room and passed them out. She told us these were good pencils that could actually be properly sharpened and "Not those decorated pencils you kids pick up everywhere these days." So I knew right away she was a complainer. And a stickler. And also somebody who wasn't sure about *these days*, even though maybe Mrs. Cryer wasn't all that old.

It was hard to tell.

She wore white shoes with thick soles, the kind a nurse might wear, and flowy flowered pants and a matching shirt. Reading glasses hung from a beaded chain around her neck. Her hair was short and straight, the kind that swung a little when she moved her head, and it was the color somewhere between white and yellow that ladies paid for. She had old hands: spotted, with big knuckles. Like my gram's hands. Or Papa's hands. Papa's hands had reminded me of tree roots, brown and big, his knuckles like knots. Even if Mrs. Cryer wasn't an *old* old teacher, I could tell by how she complained about our fun pencils that she thought she was old, and that old meant right and young meant wrong. Papa used to say that that kind of attitude would make you old more than years would, but even he had only listened to the oldies radio station.

Mrs. Cryer passed out the new composition books. She passed out the new pencils. The points were sharp and the erasers were as fresh as a puppy's nose. Our desks were clustered into groups. There weren't a lot of us in summer school. It was mostly the usual suspects, like me. There was Silas, who collected banana stickers at lunch and then spent most of the afternoon shouting, "Banana!" except when he was shouting, "Infected!" That's what kids yell during Infection, which is a kind of tag but not the same as zombie tag. There was Cameron, who got stressed out a lot. Anytime we did group work or moved around to sit in another person's seat, he hated it. He hated sitting in someone else's spot, and he hated letting someone sit in his. In kindergarten, he used to cry about it. He didn't cry about it anymore, but we all knew it was an issue, even if the teachers didn't, and they always wondered why our workstations didn't rotate the way they'd planned. There was Eddie and Ivy, who were cousins and also my friends, and Madison said only one of them had failed the state test and the other one was there just because they didn't like to be separated. I didn't think that was true, but I didn't know for sure. Madison sat right next to me. She never got in trouble. Her desk was neat and orderly. Her papers were never wrinkled or torn. Her name was never on the board for owing an assignment. Even her hair was smooth and her part always perfectly straight. Her handwriting was so good that if Madison was in your class, that's all you'd ever hear about. Her beautiful handwriting. If the teacher had a Penmanship Club for perfect spelling tests in perfect cursive handwriting, Madison was the first to earn a spot. I peeked over at the nameplate on her composition book where she'd signed her name. *Madison*. It was like a grown-up wrote out of her kid hand.

Mrs. Cryer said the new composition books were for free-writing. It didn't matter what we wrote as long as we did it and it was to warm up our brains and get us ready for the day. The first writing prompt was written in green marker on the whiteboard. *How I spent my summer vacation...*

No one was buying it.

Eddie raised his hand and asked, "Are you kidding me?" He tipped his chair back on two legs. "What summer vacation?"

Ivy tipped her chair back on two legs, too. That's how it worked with Eddie and Ivy.

Mrs. Cryer did that signal that means *Four on the floor*, and then she made a face that said *Right now* and Eddie and Ivy both thunked down. Mrs. Cryer said, "It's a classic writing prompt. And you did have two weeks from the end of the school year until now."

Eddie crossed his arms. "That's not a summer vacation."

"It's what many adults get for a vacation," said Mrs. Cryer.

Ivy said, "But we're kids."

"It's good practice for the real world, which is how you should think about school. Summer school is your job now."

Everybody groaned.

Sticking up my hand, I spoke before she called on me. "But this isn't the real world. It's school. For kids."

She sighed big. I knew that sigh. A lot of people sighed like that around me. She waved her hand to the green prompt on the board. "Nevertheless. And please wait to be called on before you speak."

"It doesn't matter," Silas said. Aside from *Banana!* and *Infected!* it was the most I'd ever heard him say. "Just look out the window."

That said it all. If you knew my town. If you did look out the window. Our classroom was on the second floor, and it used to be that when you looked out the window at just the right spot, you could see the silver flashing of the lake. But the water wasn't visible anymore. And the lake wasn't anything a person wanted to look at, now that it had been drained and was all shallow and muddy and swampy. Most businesses were closed or never opened for the season, and the tourists weren't going to show up. The rentals and motels signs read VACANT all the time. The streets were empty, except for the summer school kids and the flocks of geese. It wasn't ever really going to be any kind of summer without the lake. Only the weather didn't know it was all different. Outside it was hot, maybe ninety degrees, and the sun was bright and yellow and there were no clouds.

"Silas is so right," Ivy said, and Eddie said, "It stinks so bad," and Silas said, "Literally. I mean, *literally* literally it stinks. The lake."

"You mean the not-lake," Ivy said, and Eddie said, "Yeah, the used-to-be-a-lake."

"There's no summer," Madison said. She'd raised her hand and kept it in the air the whole time she spoke. "We're in school. The lake's gone. This is one rotten summer vacation."

I'd kind of expected her to agree with the teacher.

Mrs. Cryer said, "Feel free to interpret the writing prompt any way you wish. It's freewriting. Brain warm-ups. Your journals are for you."

No one believed that, since she'd also said she'd collect them every few days to look over.

Max shot his hand in the air. "I'm going to write about what I *wish* I was doing over my summer vacation."

"Yes," Mrs. Cryer said. "That's the spirit!"

That first day of lousy summer school, everybody leaned over their journals like they were all set to go and knew exactly what they were going to write about. Not me. I held my pencil up. I knew how to fake it. I leaned over the desk and curved my other arm around my notebook as if I was going to stop somebody from copying.

Mrs. Cryer settled into her desk chair and the room was filled with the soft scritching and shushing noises of everybody else's new summer school pencils moving over the pages of their brand-new summer school journals, and even though I got tired of sitting that way I didn't budge, except to wiggle my pencil every now and then. The page was smooth and white and undisturbed, like fresh snow before anyone's gone out in it or the lake's surface on a calm morning (back before), and I didn't want to mess it up.

Chapter 3

I walked home with Ivy and Eddie. It wasn't a long walk, but it was a hot one. All a person had to do was step out of air-conditioning to break a sweat. Waves of heat shimmered over the parking lot blacktop.

Just knowing the water in the lake was gone made it feel even hotter. We all felt it. I could see it in the way the kids ran out of the building and headed to the buses, how they ran until the heat smacked them, and then, knowing that there was nothing out there for us but that heat, hardly had the energy to get to the bus circle or head on home. There was no buzz from the motorboats, no loud Jet Skis, no people laughing and calling out. There was no afternoon at the public beach, or hanging off a dock, or a boat ride after parents were off work, and now not only was there not enough water for a motorboat, your parents were probably too stressed about how business was down everywhere to even think about doing anything fun. With no lake, it was only AC if you had it, or a kiddie pool in the backyard, or a sprinkler, which was always freezing cold and never as much fun as you think it will be, or a homemade "Slip 'N Slide" in the yard made out of garbage bags, and then you'll just get in trouble for using them all up. The smell was all wrong, too. Silas was right when he said it stank. It did. The water was mucky and it smelled like decay. There was no smell of swimsuits, sunscreen, and gasoline, which probably sounds like a gross combination but it's not. It's the best. It's the smell of summertime and vacation.

The main road curved around the lake. Summer houses and rentals and condos were built right up on the edge of the lake with docks sticking in all over the place like a bar graph gone wrong. The main part of the town was on the other side of the road, all except for the famous restaurant that didn't even have a parking lot, just rows of docks on the lake side. There were a couple diners and pizza places, stores to buy souvenirs and ball caps, a little grocery store, one laundromat, some places to get your car fixed, boat storage, RV storage, a dollar store, the little museum where my grandmother volunteered, and the building that was the town hall and fire station. The fire department was all volunteer and they had one truck and one ambulance. Farther out was the public marina and then the path to the small beach that was a state park. Park workers raked the goose poop out of the dark sand—which was more like dirt than anything else—every morning. There was no lifeguard and lots of signs about swimming at your own risk, some warnings posted about toxic algae, and now a sign that just said CLOSED. Back from the main street were a few more streets and was where I lived, and then civilization petered out the farther you got from the water. After the Amish furniture store and the trailer park there wasn't any place to go except into the cornfields and the east-west interstate lined with warehouses, fast-food places, and truck stops.

Across the lake was another small town, but it was farther off the water. There were small canals that were almost like boat driveways, and marinas, too, across the quarter-mile of water, and restaurants on the lakefront.

Eddie, Ivy, and I were the only people walking down the sidewalks, and there were hardly any cars, which was not how it ever was. I'm not counting the geese, which had pretty much taken over. If there was a traffic jam these days it wasn't tourists, it wasn't people in swimsuits and beach towels dragging in the road as they tried to cross the street, it was a parade of slow geese. I don't even know why geese had wings. If you had wings, why wouldn't you fly across the road? I didn't get it. We did our best to avoid the goose poop, but it was pretty much impossible.

Eddie kicked a rock down the sidewalk in front him as though he were playing soccer, stopping every now and then to pluck some clover for Ivy, who was trying to braid it as she walked.

"Bracelets?" I asked.

"Goose crowns," she answered.

"Ugh," I said.

Most of the seasonal places hadn't opened this summer since the governor had ordered the lake drained. Sycamore Lake is a man-made lake about six miles long with an old, earthen dam, and every year engineers came out to inspect it. This year was the year they said the whole dam—the whole edge of the lake, nearly all the way around—was in danger of collapse. They said things like *imminent failure* and *tidal wave of mud*. The spillway at the far end of the lake was opened and the lake drained down to about two or three feet of water. The engineers and the governor said if they hadn't done it there would have been a tsunami of water and mud that could swallow the whole town in less than half an hour. That's why another thing you see around here are blue signs with arrows that say EVACUATION ROUTE.

Now it was nearly a swamp, which is what it used to be over a hundred years ago before people turned it into a lake.

The draining happened right after my grandfather died. Papa. Except unlike Papa, it was on the news. Papa wasn't on the news. His obituary in the paper didn't count. Papa was a private sadness that everybody forgot I was carrying. My teachers and my friends forgot. And the people who knew I was sad were sad, too.

But the lake was everybody's sadness.

After the lake was drained like a bathtub, everybody said how Sycamore Lake was a ghost town, all muddy and swampy and little bit stinky, and with no tourists. The mayor and the village council and everybody worried it would stay a ghost town. I thought that was a strange way to put it because they meant ghost as in *empty*, but to me ghosts felt like something that kept me company. Not the scary kind or the Halloween kind or the movie kind, but the kind that live with you. The kind that remind you of things you've done and the way things used to be and the people you've loved who are gone and the people who've changed.

The hot walk home after summer school wouldn't be so bad if we could stop at the Frozen Fish, which was an ice-cream stand, but even that was closed. The sign said the same thing it had since October: CLOSED FOR THE SEASON. REASON? FREEZING!

Eddie pointed at the sign and Ivy shouted, "It's not freezing!" And then together they yelled, "We all scream for ice cream!"

Orange picnic tables were shoved up against the building and grass grew up through the cracks in the pavement. Some fluffy goslings walked around on their tall legs. They looked cute, but we knew better. There were warnings on the news about it: "The Department of Natural Resources is reminding people today that it is nesting season, and to stay away from any geese, as they will be more aggressive than normal."

We walked through the empty and lonely downtown, past the turn to our houses, and to the public park with a beach (empty) and the boat launch (also empty). We looked at the hole where the lake used to be. It was swampy. Shallow. Full of weeds. The mud was thick and dark and the water didn't start for ages.

The stubby grass was covered in greenish goose poop, and we climbed up to the top of an old wooden picnic table to stay out of the way of the geese that crowded the shore. If we shifted our weight around, we could make the rickety table rock like a surfboard.

Eddie had a pocketful of rocks and chucked one toward the water, but it skittered on the muddy beach and made a goose honk and flap its wings. Maybe he was aiming for the water—which he could never hit, not now—but he started aiming at the geese.

"Stop," I told him. "That's mean."

Ivy said, "They've pooped all over our beach. That's what's mean. We'll never get it back. They'll think it's theirs forever. Even after the water comes back. If it ever does." She crushed up the clover crowns and flung them out into the grass. "Some people say that if we ever get water again, it will be bad. You know, with the algae that grows."

Eddie said we might end up like that lake that was a few hours away. Swimming had been banned there for years. "Because the water stays so warm and chemicals from the farms get washed into it. It's toxic. Poison."

Ivy and Eddie are first cousins and there are a hundred different ways they are the same. They are the same height. They stand the same way, squared up and ready, on their toes. Their backpacks are different colors but the same size, the same brand, and from the same store. Eddie is a boy, though, and Ivy is a girl, and Eddie has short dark hair and dark skin, and Ivy has long yellow hair and the kind of white skin like mine that is pretty much always pink, whether it's from sun or exertion or emotion. Eddie wears a camo ball cap as much as he's allowed, and Ivy always has hair elastics up her wrist like bracelets.

They act like they're brother and sister, but because they're cousins and don't live in the same house they're like siblings that don't ever fight like siblings so it's better.

I'll never be as close to anybody as Eddie and Ivy are to each other. Maybe Papa, but he was my grandfather. Probably Hank, even though he's a dog. But Papa was gone now and so was Hank. My mom's going to have a baby soon so I'll have a sister or a brother, but that won't be the same thing at all. There will be nearly twelve years between me and the baby, and that's a lot.

When Mom and Dad told me we were having a baby, they gave me that speech about how a heart grows and there is always more love and having a new baby in the family didn't mean they'd love me any less. I already knew how it worked. I didn't think they would love me less, but then sometimes I couldn't help but wonder. Why would they even bring it up? Why were they thinking about loving anybody less? It got me wondering, what my parents thought about when they were thinking about me. Crumpled up school papers crammed into my backpack. Always late with notes from the school. My laundry basket still filled with clean clothes and my dirty ones all heaped on the floor. Back talk. Lousy test grades. Summer school. What happened with Hank. What happened before that.

Eddie said, "The geese will probably still be here, even if

the lake is ruined forever." He stood like a baseball pitcher on the top of the wobbly table with a rock, ready to throw.

I said, "I just don't want to get attacked. Geese will attack."

Ivy said, "Remember how they chased that news crew? After one of those lake press conferences? They ripped up that lady's skirt. The camera person threw a shoe at them."

Eddie said, "I'll save the rocks for our escape, then."

Somewhere across the lake a dog barked. It sounded familiar, but dog barks were tricky like that. Did it sound like Hank? I waited for the dog to howl and I thought I might howl, too, in solidarity, but the dog just barked regular a couple more times and then after a bit the geese started honking and flapping their wings, and when we left, Eddie divided his rocks up between the three of us, for our protection.

They were warm from Eddie's pockets and the hot weather that wouldn't quit. I clutched mine in my fists but I didn't think I could actually throw them at a goose, even if it was attacking me, even if I had to choose, me or the goose. I didn't know what I thought about that.

How I spent my summer vacation
—Noah Pham

What I did for my summer vacation: not sleep late, feed the dog, scratch the dog behind the ears, wait for the bus (for forever), bring a lot of recess stink in first thing in the morning because it was already hot out and the bus was even hotter and it was stinky, too, filled with stinky high school students, then make a grand entrance and see that Max is the only other kid from my town at this summer school. I can't believe we're the only two who ended up here.

What I wish I did for my summer vacation: anything but this.

Chapter 4

After we escaped from the geese, Eddie and Ivy went their way and I went mine. I stopped by Gram's house. It's a ranch, just like my house, but closer to the water. Gram's house is white with pale blue shutters and has a giant oak tree out front that she complains about because of acorns and the squirrels that were always climbing all over it and jumping onto the roof.

The house was closed up and dark, but I knew Gram was in there by the way the blue light of the TV flickered. I stuck my face up to the screen on the front door to look through the window. I couldn't see what she was watching. A court show? A cooking show? The news? Probably the weather. She watched weather reports all day, as though their true purpose was to convince her to stay inside.

I knocked and leaned on the doorbell. Mom said it was rude. Just give a person a minute, she said. But this way Gram would know it was me. And I guess if she knew it was me, she also knew she didn't have to answer.

The closed up and quiet house made me sad.

When Papa was alive, I'd stop by and have an after-school snack or watch TV with them or be with the dogs, or just Hank, when we still had Hank. Hank was one of Papa's foster dogs. Hank was the kind of dog that was a lot like me—mostly normal, except when we weren't, and when we weren't it was a big problem.

Hank's thing was that he pretty much didn't do doorways, which maybe doesn't sound too bad until you start thinking about all the doorways there are on the way to someplace, any place. Whenever Hank left the house it was a big deal. Only Papa could coax him in or out. Otherwise, Hank cowered. Inside the house he stayed in the open spaces of the living room and kitchen. He never went into any of the other rooms in the house because he wasn't going to go through the doorway. Everybody loved Hank and everybody got exasperated with him, too. I knew exactly what it was like.

Some of Papa's foster dogs were regular old dogs who acted in all the regular dog ways and some had issues. Some of Papa's dogs had never gone for a walk and would just stand on the sidewalk, not knowing what to do. There had been a couple dogs that didn't even know how to eat food out of a dog bowl and some that couldn't eat with anyone in the room. The thing about foster dogs, Papa always said, was that you'd never know the reason why a dog was scared or mad or whatever, all you knew was that they were. The why of it didn't matter. It was just who that dog was. And all a person could do was accept it and love the dog and help the dog out. Papa was good at that. If he couldn't help a dog out—or change the dog's behavior— he always still loved it, and Papa said that's what love was.

We didn't know why Hank didn't go through doorways and we never would. All we needed to know was that he didn't. "And Hank's never going to tell us," Papa said, cool as a cucumber because that's who he was, never rattled by the surprises his foster dogs carried.

Hank didn't do doorways but he did about everything else. He played fetch. He was good with a Frisbee. He caught snowballs, and even though Papa said he was a smart dog, Hank was surprised every time one burst apart in his mouth. He liked to get out on the water in a boat or a canoe. He didn't even seem annoyed by his doggy life jacket the way some dogs were. He didn't like doorways, but he liked people, and he liked me. We'd curl up on the floor and watch cooking shows with Gram or play outside when Papa got him out the back door.

Once in a while, Papa had a mean foster dog. Papa said it was because the dogs didn't know any other way. He told me that sometimes anger was a survival skill. "That anger is what kept them alive. That anger in them, that's the part that knows they deserve better. My job is to show them that they don't need it anymore." Our job was to accept the foster dogs, mysteries and all.

Gram's sadness was no mystery. It was grief. It was ghosts. Mom said that Gram was tough as nails, and sharp as them, too, sometimes, but that didn't mean she wasn't hurting.

These days, without Papa and without foster dogs, the only sounds at Gram's were house noises. Creaky doors. The scrape of oak branches over the low roof. The hum of the television, always on, in the living room or in Gram's bedroom. Used to be people talked in her house. Gram and Papa. Used to be, there were dogs snuffling in the living room, whining in their sleep, and dogs barking outside.

Part of that quietness and loneliness was my fault.

When there was no answer at Gram's, I went home. Mom and her big belly (she said it wasn't really even that big yet) sat at the kitchen table, her cell phone handy in case anyone emailed about a vacation rental (no one did), peeling an orange. I poured myself the last of the lemonade and started mixing more from the powder mix, which Gram said wasn't as good as the real stuff and Papa had said how anything's good on a hot day and Mom said how the mix was easy to make. But Gram was right. The homemade stuff is great.

Mom had her feet propped on the chair across from her. They were swollen and she liked to keep them up. She asked, "So how was school? Want to share my orange?"

I said, "Same old," and "No, thanks." It felt wrong. Like taking food from the baby. "Where's Dad?"

"Pulling docks out. He hired some guys from the marina. I'd offer to help him but, you know," she said, patting her belly.

People about lost their minds when they got letters saying that all the docks had to be taken out of the water for the dam repair. The notice said the docks would have to be out by a certain date or the construction crews would do it, and then the owners would get charged for it because the docks were in the way of the repairs. Dad had just started working a nightshift at one of the big shipping warehouses up by the highway, and now all of a sudden he had this big job to do that ate up his days.

My parents are property managers for rentals around the lake. They take the bookings and collect the money and do the maintenance and the cleaning and all that. They don't own the places—that's some rich person who lives somewhere else—but they wished they did. They were saving up to get some rentals of their own, and they talked at night about how maybe things would be dirt cheap and then talked about how no one was selling because they wouldn't get any money, so all the sellers were waiting until next year, when maybe the dam would be repaired and the water would be back and everything would be worth more money, which was good news for people with money. They each used to have a job and we had two paychecks but with so little for them to do except pull out docks and make sure mice didn't move in, it had been cut back to one job they shared. Mom and Dad acted as though this was fine—Mom could (mostly) go on a long maternity leave and rest through the heat of the summer—but I knew they didn't like it.

"Do you think anyone is coming at all this summer?"

"Probably not."

I told her I stopped by Gram's on the way home but that Gram didn't answer. Mom looked sad and told me it was nice of me to try. "I can't stand it," I said. "Gram doesn't even have Hank to keep her company."

Mom just shook her head. She'd been over this with me before. I didn't care about all the things she was right about, which was most of it—all the ways Hank was too much for Gram right now, even if she loved him—all that mattered was that Gram was sad and lonely.

"If it weren't for me, Hank would still be there."

"Lolo. You know that's not true."

"It's mostly true." Then, because Mom looked sad and tired and worried, I told her about Mrs. Cryer. Not all of it, of course. Just the interesting parts. "You'll never guess who the summer school teacher is."

She pretended to think. "The mayor? The governor?"

"The Statue of Liberty from the Sycamore Lake Boat Parade."

"Belinda Cryer?"

"Her name's *Belinda*? You *know* her?" Sure, I'd known Mrs. Cryer was Sycamore Lake famous, but I didn't think that my mom actually knew her. "From the papers, right?"

"I don't know. It's a small town. And I did know she was a teacher. Your dad might have had her. Ask when he gets home."

"Wait. Was Dad trouble? Do you think she knows who I am? Because my dad was a juvenile delinquent?"

Mom laughed. "I don't think he was a juvenile delinquent, Lo."

"Right. As if anyone would ever tell me."

Chapter 5

The next morning of summer school we were back to our journals. We had ten minutes of freewriting, which was both too much (because I didn't want to do it) and not enough time (even if I could come up with something to write, wouldn't it take me a while?). I opened my black-and-white composition notebook. I turned from the first blank page to the second blank page.

The topic was written on the board.

I was brave when...

I wasn't brave. I've never been brave.

Mrs. Cryer said, "It's just some freewriting to warm up our brains. Just keep your pencil moving. Don't worry about mistakes."

I wondered if anybody believed her. You didn't get to go to summer school because no one was worried about your mistakes. You were in summer school because it was *all about* the mistakes.

Everybody else leaned in over their journals and got to work. What had they all been brave about? How did they know right away what it was? I got into my writing fake-out pose, but Mrs. Cryer came over to my desk, suspicious, and peered over my shoulder at my blank page.

I said, "I've got to think." Which wasn't true. There was

nothing to think of. Because the one time I'd tried to do something brave I only made everything worse. And I hadn't even been thinking about being brave, anyway. The only thing I'd been thinking about then was sadness and animal control.

Mrs. Cryer said I should think and write at the same time. "Even if you write *I don't know what to write*. Or the prompt, over and over. Okay? Or you can flip it, the way we did yesterday, and write about the opposite." Maybe Mrs. Cryer was trying to be nice to expand my writing choices, but the opposite of brave is cowardly, so I wasn't so sure.

She was all friendly smiles but I didn't like it. What made her think I wasn't brave?

Chapter 6

Back in March and a week after Papa's funeral, Hank was stuck outside in Gram's backyard, and he howled and howled.

That sad howl was how I felt inside, and I thought, if I were a dog, I'd howl like that, too.

I couldn't bear Hank's sadness a moment longer. I didn't even think about how it was the middle of the night and it was dark out, and I wasn't supposed to go anywhere without telling my parents. Maybe that was brave. I don't know. I climbed out of bed. I shoved my feet into flip-flops. My "Dog tired" nightgown was as long as a dress so I didn't change clothes. At the front door, I waited to see if my parents heard me, but the only sound was Hank howling out his broken heart. Curling my toes in so my flip-flops wouldn't flop, I slipped out the front door and then scuffed down the deserted sidewalk. Gram's house was one block away and one block over. Porch lights and streetlights showed my way. This was back before the lake was drained and there was still water, and the slosh of it against the dam and the docks was a familiar and comforting sound.

At Gram's house, the bright light shone from the front of the garage but the house was all dark and quiet. I creaked open the chain-link gate to the backyard. It's a pretty big yard with a fence and three big doghouses that Hank would never go in and Gram's tomato garden. There's a big maple tree that makes good shade most of the day. It wasn't a bad place to be, except if your heart is broken. If your heart is broken any place is a bad place to be.

Up close, the howling ran right through me. When I called out, "Hank? Here, Hank," I was actually surprised regular words came out and I didn't bark or howl right back at him.

Hank stood under the tree where it was extra dark. His coat was brown and white, and so I saw the bits of white, and then I knew for sure when he howled again.

"I know. I know."

I edged toward him and held out my hand so it would get to Hank's snout before the rest of me, and he could sniff it for the one millionth time, the way I'd been taught.

"It's me, Hank. It's Lolo."

Hank didn't care. He kept on howling. I reached slowly, slowly, to Hank's collar and tugged him forward. Hank didn't move. I didn't pull hard. Hank was mostly mutt but maybe enough terrier that a person could tell. A medium-sized dog with short white-and-dark-brown fur. He was solid and strong with perfect triangular dog ears. Papa used to pick him up and carry him just like he was a little dog. Hank usually never minded but I didn't dare try it. I talked soft dog-talk, soft dog-love talk, and tugged again and again and Hank moved forward an inch or two.

"I'm sorry, Hank," I said. And, "You can do it. Come on. You're doing great. Almost there."

It was a long way across the yard. Then the back deck.

Hank went up the three steps without any trouble. The same for across it. The trouble started after I slid open the unlocked back door.

Hank shivered and shook and dropped low. He stopped howling and switched to whining. If you think that howling broke my heart, the whining was worse.

Hank was always with Papa when he went in or out of the house, and I'm just me. I'm no dog whisperer. Hank wouldn't budge. I pushed his rump. I tried talking the way Mom spoke to the baby in her belly, all soft and sweet. "It's okay, Hank. It's okay. Gram's in there. You need Gram. Gram needs you."

Hank whined. When I pushed on Hank's rump again he scooched forward, just a little, just enough for me to think maybe it would happen. Hank would go through the doorway. I'd be the one who helped him. "That's a good puppy, that's a good puppy, come on now."

"Who's there?" Creaky like an old rocking chair that never rocked, Gram's voice called out from somewhere in the dark house.

"It's me, Gram. Lolo. Lolo and Hank." I squinted into the darkness. The sliding back door opened into the kitchen. I couldn't see anything.

"You're letting the bugs in, Lo. Close the door. I don't want mosquitos in here."

"Hank won't stop howling."

Nothing.

"He hurts, Gram."

In the house, it was darkness and silence.

"Gram?"

"Oh, Lolo, what can I do with that dog?"

"Just let him in. You need each other. He's stuck out here."

"Lolo. You need to leave it alone. Go on home."

Mom said that Gram was angry in her sadness and sometimes that's what happened. A person feels what a person feels. Of course she's sad, Mom said. We're all sad. Of course she's angry. Mom said we're all a little bit angry.

"Dogs get broken hearts, too," I told Gram. "Papa always said. Hank needs you."

I still couldn't see her. There was a dark shape that was maybe her or was really the refrigerator. I couldn't tell. And her harsh voice didn't help Hank, who planted his backside down and still shivered. I slid my arm around him but it didn't make any difference.

Gram said, "Take him to your house."

"He doesn't want me." I left out the part how I didn't even think I could get Hank through the fence gate, never mind down the street where there were only more doors to get through. Here, there was just the one doorway. "Hank wants you."

"I can't." Gram sniffled. "Leave that dog be. You're scaring him to pieces."

"He's howling and howling." I thought about what Papa might do when he was at his wit's end. How he'd tuck Hank into his chest and pick him up and give him treats, and how somehow, sometimes, Hank didn't mind doors that way. At least not with Papa. My dad had tried it, the day of the funeral, and Hank had been all growls, clear that it wasn't going to happen.

I told Gram, "Somebody's going to call animal control. You can't let him go back to a shelter. Do you have any hot dogs? Hot dogs might get him in."

Gram made a funny sound. A snort or a laugh or a cry. Without seeing her, I couldn't tell which it was. Then Gram stepped to where there was a sliver of bright white light from the security lights. She wore a blue, sleeveless, flowery night-gown and her short gray hair stuck out every which way. She raised her arm. I thought maybe she was going to signal for Hank, do that thing Papa did, snapping his fingers with his hand at his leg, or offer a treat. Or maybe she was even going to reach for Hank's collar. That's not what she did. She reached forward, thunked the sliding door closed, and locked it.

Startled, Hank yipped and pushed back. My knees hurt from pressing into the wood of the deck. "Sorry," I said to Hank. "I thought I could help."

Hank looked at me, quiet, his dark eyes shining, and for one moment I thought maybe I had actually accomplished something, but he started howling all over again.

I don't know why I thought it was ever a good idea. I wasn't like Papa. I didn't know what Papa did, and now I never would. I didn't get things done. I couldn't even convince my grand-mother to help.

So I gave up.

"Good night then, Hank. I'm sorry." I scratched behind one of his perfect ears and rested my head on his for a moment until he shook me off to howl some more.

When I left I latched the gate behind me, even though it didn't matter. Hank would never go through it. I listened to Hank howl all the way back home. It wasn't long before other neighborhood dogs started up again.

A window screeched up and someone stuck their head out and hollered, "Call off your dog! Call off your dog!" and it only made all the other dogs louder. Any other time I could have figured out exactly who it was, who could be so mean. I live in a small place. It's just a village and a lake, when it wasn't summer and there weren't tourists, and everyone knew about Papa and his foster dogs and everyone knew Papa had died.

I hollered right back. "Leave him be!" Then I ran. I lost a flip-flop and stubbed my toe on the uneven sidewalk.

The angry neighbor shouted, "I'm calling animal control!"

And then I wasn't sad anymore. I wasn't thinking of Hank. I was filled with anger. Just like Gram. I kicked away my other stupid flip-flop. They were summer shoes. There wasn't going to be a summer, there wasn't going to be a lake, and Mom always said they weren't real shoes anyway. I yelled over all the dogs barking. "Do it! Do it! I dare you! No one's going to blame that dog for crying!"

I ran home barefoot.

**

That next morning after I'd tried to get Hank in the house, I was back at Gram's with cut-up hot dogs and pepperoni. They were the treats Papa used when things got really bad with Hank. Mom went over with me, too. We all looked like we rolled out of bed but especially Gram, who was still in her fuzzy bathrobe.

Hank snuffled around Gram's feet and woofed as though he had a lot of questions we couldn't answer, and when he started up on a sad howl Gram reached down to rub his ears.

I fed him some treats but after the first couple of bites Hank wasn't interested in any of it. I didn't know if that made him a smart dog, a dumb dog, or a full dog. For sure he was a stuck dog.

I ate one of the slices of pepperoni, since cold hot dog was never very good. "See?" I said to Hank. "Yum."

Gram sat down right on the deck steps even though she was in her bathrobe. Hank, tired, snuffled up into Gram's lap. Gram said, "Poor guy. He's exhausted from barking all night." I didn't say anything about how she hadn't helped at all with that. She rubbed Hank's soft ears and said how he was a good boy, such a good boy, the very best boy, what was she going to do without him.

I asked what she was talking about.

Mom told me to leave it.

I asked, "Remember that foster dog who liked cucumbers? Do you have any cukes, Gram?" Cukes is what Papa called them. "Hank's pretty good right now. I bet we could get him inside. All three of us."

"Lo," my mom said in that voice that was steady, serious, and had some things to explain. "Getting Hank in the house is only a temporary solution."

"There are doggy litter boxes. Did you know that? Not just piddle pads. But litter boxes. I bet I could even make one."

"Oh, good grief, Lo," Mom said.

Gram, her arms all full of Hank, said, "I've already called Michelle."

"What? No." Michelle was the foster dog lady. She drove an old minivan practically made of dog hair, she always smelled like dog food, and I was pretty sure every pair of socks she owned had dog pictures on them. She was the one who kept track of all the rescue dogs and placed them in foster homes and found them forever homes.

Mom said how it wasn't my decision.

"*Mom*. Gram needs Hank. What's she supposed to do without Hank? It'll all be too much without Hank. Gram just said! She said how lonely she'd be without him. She can't lose Hank *and* Papa."

Next thing I knew, there was a lonely howl from Hank and the bang of the door closing. Gram had up and left us again. The blinds at the big glass door swept across, shutting us out and shutting her in.

Mom said, "How about we have some compassion and patience right now."

"For Hank?"

"For *Gram*."

***

Gram's blinds were still closed up when I said goodbye to Hank a couple of days later.

Hank snuggled in as if he knew it was goodbye or as if he could smell my sadness, because dogs can do that. All I could smell was his fur. I told Hank Gram sure could use some of his love right now, even though Mom and Dad said about a hundred times how caring for a dog like Hank was too much for Gram. No one said anything about how it was my fault Hank was on the wrong side of Gram's back door.

Mom had come with me. She told me Hank's new foster home was just across the lake. As if that was supposed to comfort me. As if that made it any better. "You know the place," she said. "That big old farmhouse kind of across the road from the marina but after the turn to the bridge. We drive by it sometimes."

"That's a horrible place for a dog," I said. "On the county route. The road's too busy. It's roadkill city."

Mom told me Michelle said it had a barn and a barn had really big doors. "That's good news for Hank, right? Maybe it will help?"

I said, "Sure." I didn't mean it. Did it mean he'd live in some old barn? How was that good? Wouldn't he be lonely? He wouldn't have Gram. He wouldn't even have me. Didn't anybody ever think about how the dogs love the people and the people love the dogs?

When I was brave
—Noah

My little brother The Brain is scared of dogs because once a dog named Sorrow (no joke) bit his knee. It didn't break the skin but left tooth-shaped purple bruises. At his house there aren't any pets but at my house there's a dog. The Brain is my half brother and The Brain says there is no way for him to be around a dog because if he's scared he can't even fake it because the dog will smell it on him and the dog will always know. They are canine lie detectors, he says. The Brain also says he admires the canine nose. He talks like that and he's only in third grade. I'm not scared of dogs even though I've also been bitten. I don't know the dog's name. I have a scar. Right on my top lip. It's a silvery slash and I've had it since I was a baby, and that's why we haven't had a pet for a while and right now I have a trial dog. I only ever want a dog. I'm a dog person. Dad got huffed up when he saw the dog at mine and mom's house, but I reminded him how I only got bit because my cousins were holding a dog that didn't want to be held and then pushed the dog into my face and it nipped.

Dad: *How do you know that? You were two years old.*
Me: *Mom told me. And I remember getting stitches because the doctor sang "How Much Is That Doggy in the Window?" while she was sewing me up.*

Dad: *Your cousins have never been very bright.*

Me: *I'm the one in summer school.*

Dad: *That test was one morning of your whole life. Don't worry about it. I went to summer school a few times because gym class wouldn't fit into my schedule and once to retake trigonometry. I just didn't get it the first time around. And then I did.*

Me: *I love that dog and that dog loves me.*

Dad: *Well, I love you, so do me a favor and don't get bit again.*

Me: *He's had all his shots. And he's not a biter. He's got other issues.*

Dad: *Everybody's got something.*

Chapter 7

Eddie's a world-class chair tipper. He says it's all about the balance. He doesn't even touch his feet to the desk legs for help. When he's tipped back, he can reach around and grab something off the desk behind him, no problem. He says it's all about the ab muscles. Core strength. He says we should do it in gym class. Chair tipping.

We were color-coding our sample test reading passages and underlining topic sentences and stuff like that, which meant nobody ever had the right color pencil and it was a good reason to get up and walk around and get the one you needed, even if you could have borrowed your neighbor's, which was Mrs. Cryer's suggestion. Summer school kids are restless. Mrs. Cryer should know that. Max said it was good to stretch your legs. He said, "Physical activity actually helps your brain," and Mrs. Cryer said, "You'll all survive until recess," and Max laughed but I wasn't sure she meant it to be funny.

On my way across the room to get a red pencil, I saw Silas making his way to the tipped-back Eddie, who was reaching for a pencil on the desk behind him. Silas had that look on his face. The one when he was about to burst out with either *Infected!* or *Banana!* So I spun back around to my desk and warned Eddie to watch out just as Silas pointed at Eddie, calling, "Infected!" and then he went on his way to the pencil sharpener.

Eddie flailed all the way down, clearing off his desk and mine in the process and sending Madison scrambling so fast she lost an entire box of colored pencils. "Some abs," said Silas, and Ivy told Silas it was his fault, and Xavier said Eddie was the one showing off, and Eddie said he was just doing what the teacher said (borrowing from a neighbor). Noah adjusted his glasses and handed some pencils that had rolled his way over to Madison, and I started collecting my test practice pages off the floor.

"That's enough now, come on people, calm it down," Mrs. Cryer ordered. When that didn't work she gave up erasing the whiteboard, handed the eraser to Noah for him to finish, and came into the scrum, stepping over our now foot-printed papers. "What did I tell you, Eddie, about keeping all four legs of your chair on the floor?"

Ivy answered. "Play stupid games, win stupid prizes."

Mrs. Cryer said, "Well, I don't think it was that *exactly*."

"I was putting it into my own words, Mrs. Cryer," Ivy said.

Mrs. Cryer said Eddie was lucky he hadn't cracked his head open. She said maybe Eddie would do better without a chair. She said she could go get a carpet square from one of the kindergarten classrooms, and half the class went, "*Burn*."

Eddie knelt on the floor and leaned onto his desk, head down, and Ivy asked, "You okay, Ed?" and he nodded, slow, and I said how it wasn't his fault.

"Silas was walking right by when Eddie fell, so maybe go get Silas a carpet square, too," I said.

"Yeah!" Ivy agreed.

"Hey!" Silas said. "That was a *coincidence.* I never touched him. And you were right there, too, Lolo, so maybe it was your fault."

Mrs. Cryer ignored us and said, "Eddie and Silas can stay with me during recess today. We can practice sitting in our chairs." She started to help pick up the mess all over the floor. The colored pencils, the test pages, our journals. When she handed a paper back to Madison, she said, "Oh my, what lovely handwriting."

"Taking away recess is the stupidest punishment ever," I said. "Everybody always needs a break. Especially in summer school."

Mrs. Cryer held a journal in her hands. It looked brand-new. The spine wasn't even cracked. "I've already decided, Willow—"

"Lolo." It was my journal.

"Yes." And then I was sure she made her voice just a little bit lower, as if she wanted to prove that my name and I were no good. "Lolo. Since I've already decided, there will be no further discussion." She didn't look at me when she said that, even though I'd already noticed she was pretty big on eye contact, as though it was a secret weapon of mind control, even though a person wasn't supposed to stare down a dog *or* kid, I figured. Mrs. Cryer flipped through my journal. She looked at the blank pages for a while, as though there was actually something there to read, as if I'd been writing with invisible ink. Then she thumped my journal down on the nearest desk. "You may stay with us, too, Lolo," she said.

"Well," I said, "maybe I may not."

"Let me rephrase. You *will* be staying with us, Lolo. Please feel free to write about how you feel about it in your journal."

Even though we got to stay inside in the air-conditioning we didn't care. Hot outside summer was better, even if it was just fifteen minutes of summertime feeling. Eddie sat just fine, all four on the floor, as Mrs. Cryer told him. Silas read a graphic novel. I tried to pretend to write in my journal, but it wasn't any easier now that Mrs. Cryer was onto me, so I made some doodles in the margins. Outside, the kids on the black-top were loud, and when they piled back into the classroom they were all sweaty and happy, and Mrs. Cryer held out her hand to me, for my journal. She looked at the doodles. She didn't buy it when I told her doodles warmed up my brain, my brain was very warmed up right now, I could take the state test this very minute.

She said, "Your brain's something, all right."

The day didn't get any better after that.

Everybody else still had recess energy and so Mrs. Cryer thought we'd all settle down if we wrote a haiku about nature.

"Okay! Brainstorming! Nature ideas!" No one answered for a little while, and so Mrs. Cryer said one of those lies teachers say without knowing they're lying. "Remember that in brainstorming there are no wrong answers."

We started making suggestions. Mrs. Cryer wrote them out in green marker. Sunsets, flowers, rain, snow, baby birds, dew on the grass. Swamps. Catfish.

I raised my hand. Since my brain was so warmed up.

Mrs. Cryer looked at me for a little while before she called on me. I guess she shouldn't have. I guess I proved her right. "Yes, Willow—Lolo?"

She turned to the board, poised to write.

Speaking carefully so she could hear how it was poetry, I said it. "Goose poop."

Mrs. Cryer didn't write it on the board so I said it again. Slowly. "Goose poop."

The class laughed. They liked it.

Mrs. Cryer still didn't write it on the board. The way the class was laughing made me say it again. "It rhymes. Goooose poooop."

Eddie and Ivy chimed in to help me out. "Inspired by nature." (Eddie.) "Haikus are nature poems. You just said." (Ivy.) "Goose! Poop! Goose! Poop! Goose! Poop!" (The rest of the class.)

Mrs. Cryer still didn't write it on the board. She took a deep breath, the cleansing kind, and said four things.

One: "Willow."

Two: "Willow, I can see that this summer will go better for you if I separate you from the other students." She pointed to an open area not far from the island that stuck out into the room, near the sink, and exiled me. I bet Mrs. Cryer didn't even think I knew the word *exile*.

"You should still be able to see the board from there."

Three: "Additionally, those words don't *really* rhyme."

Four: "It's also inappropriate."

On our walk home after school, Eddie and Ivy tried to say how it wasn't so bad, exile. More space, they said. Closer to the pencil sharpener, Ivy said. Closer to the door, Eddie said, which made my day probably, like, thirty seconds shorter than anyone else's.

I said if goose poop was inappropriate, somebody needed to tell the geese.

"For sure," Ivy said.

Eddie stopped walking and stood at attention, sticking one arm up in the air.

I asked, "What are you doing?"

"I'm Mrs. Cryer," he answered. "Can't you tell? I'm the Statue of Liberty. I'm the Statue of Liberty in the boat parade."

"You'd think," Ivy began, "that someone who's famous for being in a boat parade wouldn't get so worked up about goose poop."

I said, "I guess it's the statue part that's important for her, not the boat parade part."

Eddie said, "Maybe she just really hates geese. My dad ate one once. A goose. For Thanksgiving. He said it tasted like beef, but also like chicken. Anyway, sorry we got you in trouble."

Ivy said, "I thought it rhymed, Lo. Just for the record. I can't believe she moved your desk like that."

"I can," I said. I always got noticed the wrong way for the wrong things.

"It was the chanting," Eddie said. "That's what got you in trouble. She should have moved all of us if she was going to move you. It's totally unfair."

I said it wasn't a big deal. I understood how the summer was going to go. Mrs. Cryer didn't like me, and I didn't like that about her.

Chapter 8

That next morning Mom had a doctor's appointment. She got to hear the baby's heartbeat at each one. She asked me sometimes if I wanted to go, but it was a long drive and the last time I was in a waiting room we were waiting for news about life and death, and so I always said no. Then I was sorry about it. It would be cool to hear the baby's heartbeat. Dad says it sounds like *swoosh swoosh, swoosh swoosh*. But even though Mom felt fine, it turned out something was wrong, and nobody knew it until Mom peed in a cup and they tested it. The doctor told her to go straight to the hospital and they told her she was probably going to have to stay there until the baby was born. Dad picked me up at school and my name got announced over the loud-speaker and I had to go to the office. The loudspeaker sounds different in summer school, maybe because the whole building is quieter and closer to empty than not.

"Willow Weaver, please come to the office with your belongings. Willow Weaver, please come to the office prepared to go home for the day."

Silas said, "Oh, you're in *trou*-ble," and I wished he'd go back to the days when he only said *Banana!* and *Infected!*

Mrs. Cryer, who had been trying to get us to organize our copies of our practice-test packets even though the page numbers hadn't printed on them, paused and looked at me, and everybody waited for me to gather up my stuff. (It wasn't much.) As I stood to leave, she said, "Don't forget your test packet," and the class called out all their *Bye*s and *See you later*s and *Lucky*s.

I swiped my journal off my desk as I packed up. I didn't want her reading any more of what I didn't write. Mrs. Cryer was full of fascinating (not) topics like "What a fish might say," "When I grow I want to be...," "A mistake I made" (as if I'd tell her), "Write your own test question" (I thought maybe we should get better at answering them first), and "Design your own hamburger" (waste of time, because the whole world knows the best burgers are at the Burger Bar, which is on the far side of the lake, and it's only open on weekends now and who even knows if they can stay in business).

Dad waited for me in the lobby at the front desk. He looked like he'd crawled straight from the lake after hauling out docks. I didn't even have time to feel embarrassed about how he wore his muddy waders to the school. His dark hair, which hung down to about his chin and was the longest hair of any dad I knew, looked flattened. My hair was like his. Mom said it matched my personality, which wasn't always one thing or the other, because my hair wasn't straight and it wasn't curly, but it could get a little wild.

"Is it the baby? Is the baby here? It's too soon for the baby. Isn't it? I'm not ready for the baby."

Dad said, "A baby's got nobody's schedule but its own."

"So it's the baby? Seriously? How's Mom?"

"Look," he said as we stepped outside into the day that was cruelly hot considering how the lake had swirled itself down the drain, "your mom's got something going on with her blood pressure and is going to have to stay at the hospital for a while."

"Going on? What's going on? And stay? For how long?"

"Don't know how long. Till it gets itself sorted out. A while. You can call her in a bit. I'm taking you over to your grandmother's. She can explain."

After Dad cleaned up and I packed we went right over to Gram's. We knocked on the front door but Dad hardly waited for her not to answer, just threw my duffel bag over his shoulder and went around to the back.

I suggested staying home on my own, but Dad said he was going to be busy and then he was going to be at his other job, and then he was going to be at the hospital with Mom.

Then I suggested staying at Ivy's or Eddie's, but Dad said we shouldn't impose, and I asked what that meant, and he said it's taking advantage of someone. I said I was pretty sure we were imposing on Gram. All Dad said was he was glad I had summer school, at least. "It will get you out of the house and give you something to do."

I wanted to say *Give me a break* but knew better.

Dad pushed open Gram's sliding back door and called, "Hello?" and Gram was right there all along in the kitchen.

"I'm making Lo some lemonade. Not like the stuff you're serving at your place."

Dad carried my bag straight back to the guest room. He

was in a hurry because he had to get to his job at the ware-house. He said the place was hot and loud, but what did you expect. He gave me a big bear hug from him and then a big bear hug that was from Mom, but it wasn't the same. Even though Dad's actually got bigger muscles, Mom is the one who hugs the hardest. She wraps her arms around me so tight and rocks me back and forth and says she just can't hug me enough, that when she hugs me she hugs baby me and now me and future me and all of me. Right now my head is just at her col-larbone. We haven't had a hug like that since the basketball that's her stomach popped out and little Chickpea Garbanzo was in the way. That's what we called the baby. It's nice. It's a family joke. Mom and Dad still hadn't said if the baby was a girl or a boy. Everything they bought for the baby was yellow and green. Gram said it would be good to have a girl so she could wear my hand-me-downs, but we didn't have them any-more. We gave them all to the church rummage sale a long time ago. Pretty much all I had left was my ratty teddy bear, all worn down and squashed, a T-shirt with glow-in-the-dark moon phases I'd loved and that I'd shoved under my mattress so Mom wouldn't give it away, and some board books.

I'd memorized them. As a little kid. So for a little while peo-ple thought I might be smart. Like, really smart. Even though books for babies are short. Probably no one ever thought how I'd go to summer school one day.

So it's Chickpea for a girl or Garbanzo for a boy. Mom and Dad won't tell me what names they're thinking of. They say it's

Chickpea or Garbanzo for real, and I tell them they should be careful because they might really talk themselves into it, and then we all laugh about it.

But now I wonder. Maybe it's not so funny. Maybe they don't know. Maybe Lolo is a weird name, after all, and Mrs. Cryer was just the first to tell me.

I said, "Say hi to Chickpea Garbanzo," and Dad finally smiled. Once, Chickpea Garbanzo punched me. Popped my hand right off Mom's belly. We were amazed and then we laughed and then we debated whether it was a foot, hand, or elbow that had done the deed, and Mom said it wasn't an elbow because the elbow was in her rib cage like she was a set of monkey bars.

Dad pulled me outside onto the deck to give me instructions for my stay at Gram's.

One: Don't cause any trouble. This was supposed to cover everything, from back talk to making my bed.

Two: Don't talk about Hank too much. (He didn't say how much was too much.)

Three: Don't drink Gram's expired milk. (Gram always said she could smell it to know if it was bad, she didn't need a date.) I had the duffel bag, my backpack, my pillow, and Dad gave me one gallon of one percent milk. Gram was too sad to take it as the personal insult she usually would.

Back in the dark kitchen, Gram said, "The baby's not being born yet."

"I know." Gram liked to explain things I already knew

sometimes. I think she thought it was educational. I tried not to take it personally because Mom said it wasn't, she's just an explainer. "It's high blood pressure," I said. I tried not to let my voice get wobbly. "Like the kind Papa always had?"

Gram did her explaining stuff again, but this time she put an arm around me as we stood by the kitchen sink and looked out the window. She smelled like lemonade and lemon dish soap both, and even though they are each lemony they are two different smells. "What she has is called preeclampsia, and it's a high blood pressure that only pregnant people get. It's supposed to mostly go away after the baby is born. The cure is the delivery of that precious little baby, but of course the doctors want the baby inside for as long as it's safe for your mom, and they want the baby out as soon as it's safe for the baby."

"How do you know so much about it? Did you have it when you were pregnant with Mom?"

Gram shook her head and answered, "I looked it up as soon as your dad called."

We stood a minute and gazed out at the backyard. I wondered how it looked to her. I thought it was as empty and strange as the drained lake without Hank. She didn't even have any tomato plants growing this summer. The dog houses were still there, but all the toys were picked up, and I'd scooped all the poop (totally rhymes) the afternoon after Michelle had taken Hank to his new foster home.

We must have both decided we didn't want to look out the window anymore, because we turned away, synchronized, and

Gram said how there was a cooking show she liked to watch now and did I have homework and go see if those were the sheets I liked on my bed.

Mom would have pulled open the curtains and peeled Gram an orange and then dumped out the expired milk before Gram had a chance to notice, but I only pulled open the curtains. The sudden summer afternoon light made me squint. Gram turned on the cooking show and sat in her chair, putting her feet up on the footstool. I sat on her flowery couch, which was too puffy to be comfortable and was kind of slippery—it gave Papa's small foster dogs all sorts of trouble because they just couldn't get up on it—and pretended I was interested in how you can't overmix biscuit dough.

Not that Gram was even paying attention. She was zoned out and only pretending to care about biscuits. She didn't even flip to the weather channel during the commercials, which was what she always did. Guess I wasn't the only faker in the family.

When Mrs. Cryer had gave us our reading logs, she said that when you spaced out in front of a screen, your brain waves were less active than if you were in a coma, but I have no idea if that's true at all or something Mrs. Cryer said to scare us. Looking at Gram right then, though, I believed it.

It was like playing zombie tag at recess. How if you got tagged, you were a zombie. You couldn't get untagged in zombie tag. You had to wait until the whole game restarted. Once you were a zombie, you stayed a zombie.

That's how I ended up on Papa's side of the closet. First I went to the guest room but there was nothing to do there but count the little wooden sheep Gram buys at craft fairs (twenty-two) and hide the one white goose with its orange beak behind the lone black-and-white cow because I'm sick of geese, and then I went to the closet in Gram's room. I stepped right in. I don't know why. Did I think it would take me somewhere where Papa's clothes didn't hang like baggy ghosts?

If a new baby or new person or pet to love makes a heart grow, what happens when a person you love is gone? When Gram's heart broke, did it shrink and lose room for the rest of us, humans and dogs?

Gram needed Papa but she couldn't have him.

She didn't need me, but here I was all the same.

What she needed was Hank.

Closing my eyes, I felt as though I was standing with Papa and smelling how his shirt pockets still smelled like dog treats, and I knew I was right. Gram needed Hank.

What I want to be when I grow up
—Noah

When I grow up I want to be a dog. I know that's not what you mean. (Where do you get these topics, Mrs. Cryer?) Every kid already has to try to answer this question when they visit their great-aunt in the nursing home. Grown-ups think it's an easy question, but it's not. My mom's a nurse at a nursing home, so believe me, I get asked this question a lot. (My mom told me once that she wants to be a cat because they don't have to answer to anyone and they sleep a lot in the sun and she doesn't have enough energy to be a dog.) You know what no one asks me? What animal I'd like to be. The answer is easy. A dog. What's it like to be a dog? How do they think? What does the world look like from dog level? What are all those smells? I want to able to smell the way a dog smells. If I could be a dog, I could help the dogs that need some TLC when I returned to my human form. I asked The Brain what animal he'd like to be and he said an ant. Seriously, The Brain? And you're supposed to be the smart one? Maybe you should pick an animal that no one will stomp on.

Chapter 9

That next morning I woke up under Gram's sailboat sheets and got my own breakfast and used the milk we brought on my cereal and had a glass of lemonade because Gram was still in her dark bedroom. I didn't exactly like it. Lemonade for breakfast. Then I went to summer school. Eddie and Ivy crowded around me and wanted to know if the baby was born and why didn't I text and said they stopped by but no one was home and how they went to Eddie's after and threw water balloons at each other. "It was fun, kind of, but not as good as swimming," Ivy said, and Eddie said, "We'll do it again sometime." Ivy asked, "So is the baby born?"

"That's not it at all." I told them what Dad and Gram had said and what Mom had said when we'd talked on the phone last night. (Mostly Mom said how it was like she was at a spa: she could rest, there was no cooking and cleaning, there was cable television but no beauty treatments, maybe she'd take up meditation. I laughed but only because I could tell she wanted me to.)

"Everything will be okay," Ivy reassured me, and Eddie said, "Yeah, Lolo. My aunt had that," and Ivy said it wasn't her mom, it was a different aunt. Silas walked by and asked if I'd been called to the office because I had been suspended, and Eddie said, "No, you jerk, her mom's in the hospital." Madison gave me a sad look.

Then it was time for the Pledge of Allegiance and morning journals. I sat faking it with my feet on the rungs of my desk and my journal tucked away on my lap until Mrs. Cryer came all the way over to me and tapped on my desk and I sat up straight.

She asked, "How's your mother, Willow?" She didn't even whisper it.

It's a small town. It's a village. Everybody knows everything, just the way people always say about places like this. Maybe Dad or Gram or Mom herself had called to tell her, because schools always want to know *Is there something going on at home we should be aware of?* like when I failed the state test after Papa died, even though I could have told you I was going to fail it anyway.

I didn't truly know the answer but I wasn't going to get into the details with Mrs. Cryer. I said, "She's fine." If I mumbled she didn't complain.

"Good," she said. "I'm glad to hear it. So you're staying with your grandmother?"

I nodded.

"Just for a little while, I'm sure."

I nodded at that, too.

"That's something to write about. It can be your entry for 'When I was brave.'"

I didn't tell her how it's not brave if you don't have a choice, it's just what you have to do, it's just what happens.

Chapter 10

Describe something green.

Mrs. Cryer had written it out in green marker on the whiteboard.

She liked green. She marked up our papers with green ink. She called it the green ink of growth, like it was something special, as if the color marking everything wrong actually mattered.

Eddie bumped my chair on the way to the pencil sharpener. It was bolted to the side of the cabinet, right over the garbage can. "Want me to sharpen yours, too?"

"No, thanks." I asked him, "What are you going to write about?"

"Money." He grinned. "You writing about goose poop?"

"Maybe," I said. Probably green goose poop was on everybody's mind now. I wondered what it would be like when Mrs. Cryer collected all our journals and she read one entry about money and then all the rest were about goose poop. I liked it. Revenge of the freewriting.

Mrs. Cryer had two signs in our classroom, aside from a smiling cartoon sun wearing sunglasses. One read MISTAKES ARE PROOF YOU ARE TRYING, and the other was a turtle with the words, YOUR SPEED DOESN'T MATTER, FORWARD IS FORWARD.

Except our speed did matter. That's the whole reason we were there. We were too slow, just like that laminated turtle taped between the two *forward*s.

Eddie sharpened a pencil for Ivy and two for Madison, and Mrs. Cryer said, "Eddie, this is my personal invitation for you to retake your seat and make your future a better place."

"Whoa," Eddie said, bumping me again on his way past. "That's heavy, Mrs. Cryer."

"This is an important summer for you students."

No one quite knew what to make of that. Maybe she expected us to agree. Maybe she didn't think we already knew. Mrs. Cryer clapped twice and turned cheery, like she could trick us into something, and said, "Let's get writing!"

I picked up my pencil. I held it over the notebook page, like I was a runner waiting for the whistle to go off, only the whistle was in my own brain and it wouldn't go off until I had an idea. All the other kids started off—some sprinted, some started slow like it was long-distance. Eddie got busy writing about money. Max laughed, so maybe he was writing about goose poop. Madison moved her pencil slowly, making her careful letters.

So I thought *green*.

I tried not to think *goose poop*.

That's how I got thinking about Papa's canoe.

***

Papa's canoe isn't green, but it makes me think about the outdoors and green grass and trees and the green stalks of cattails at the edge of the lake. Papa's canoe is as yellow as the summer sun and is sleek and shiny. When the sun shines on it, it almost hurts to look at. It's made of Kevlar. That means it looks like plastic but it's not. It's tough but it's also light enough for me to carry.

It's different from a regular canoe. It's aerodynamic and as fast as a kayak. Papa used a kayak paddle with it, not a canoe paddle. A canoe paddle has a paddle on only one end, and a kayak paddle has paddles on both ends, so when you're paddling with a kayak paddle you dip down on one side and then the other and go, go, go, instead of switching the paddle back and forth from side to side. The seat is low, which is another way it's different from a regular canoe. It's a rectangle of Styrofoam stuck right on to the bottom as a seat. It's pretty much like sitting right on the water. There's a wooden bar, also wrapped in Styrofoam, for a backrest. In a regular kind of canoe you sit up on a seat.

The canoe's a one-seater but plenty of times Papa would take a dog out with him. Hank didn't like doorways, but he had no problem scrabbling into the canoe and wearing a doggy life jacket and sitting between Papa's knees or stretching out low in the front. Or reach his head out and sniff all the lake smells, leaning into the good ones and then sitting up and barking.

Because the canoe was light it was really meant for canoe adventures, like portage, which is when you have to carry your canoe from one body of water to another, but we didn't have anything like that around here. What it meant for around here was that Papa carried the shiny yellow canoe out from the dusty detached garage, across the street, down the grassy bank, and to the shore.

I thought about that canoe. Left behind in the spider-webby garage. How I bet Gram never even thought about it and I bet Hank did, if dogs think like that.

I thought about how the canoe wasn't heavy at all and how the lake was shallow.

I didn't write it all down exactly like that. Or at all. How could I? It was too personal to write about.

But I did write about something green that morning in my journal. I wrote so lightly it was almost like invisible ink.

Green goose poop in green grass by the green lake is green.

That's what I wrote.

So I wasn't feeling too bad that day. It felt like I'd gotten started. But then what happened happened.

Describe something green
—Noah

Shallow water lake
Geese take over, green goose poop
It is everywhere

Chapter 11

When what happened happened it was the afternoon, nearly the end of the day, and we were adding circles to the bodies of our reading caterpillars. Every twenty minutes of reading got us a new circle to glue to the caterpillar and then we got to choose a piece of candy for every circle. All the caterpillars were hung on the wall above the bookshelves. Max said we were too old for this, but Mrs. Cryer said you're never too old for a reading caterpillar or reward candy and I still wasn't going to like her.

I read about kids who survived dangerous things and about a dog that traveled in time and a whole series about foster dogs, and Silas flicked the cover of one of the books on my desk and said, "I read those, like, two years ago," and I said, "I like them. Go away." Eddie got in Silas's face and said, "Lolo likes dogs, okay?" and Ivy said, "She loves dogs, got it?" and Silas said, "Woof woof." When I returned one of the dog books to the shelf far across the room, Noah Pham ran to grab it as though he was waiting for it, the way kids used to fight over the graphic novels about dog superheroes in the school library. Silas used to cry about those books, when they were all checked out, when we were in the first grade. You never saw a kid cry with so much booger production.

We were scribbling glue sticks and growing our caterpillars. Silas, whose caterpillar had alternating orange and blue circles only, started in on how his reward candy was missing. He went around the room, asking if anyone had seen his lollipops. He had the second-longest caterpillar and the second-most amount of candy, mostly lollipops.

"Silas," Mrs. Cryer said, "this is quiet reading time." She was at the back of the room stapling completed caterpillars to the bulletin board and looked at him over her shoulder. "You need to be quiet and you need to be reading."

"Mrs. Cryer, there's, like, seven minutes of school left today, and my candy is gone."

"Your candy is gone?"

"Yeah," he answered. "It was in my desk. I'm missing, like, eight lollipops, Mrs. Cryer."

"Whoa," Noah said, impressed. "That's a lot of twenty minutes."

Eddie tried to get up to count Silas's circles to see if it was true, but Mrs. Cryer pointed at him and said, "Plant it," and he did, even as he said, "It's a *math* problem, Mrs. Cryer. It's real-world math." Mrs. Cryer ignored him.

I only had one or two lollipops, and they were deep in my desk. They weren't big lollipops. They weren't special ones— they weren't swirly and they didn't have bubble gum or anything inside. They were just ordinary little suckers.

Mrs. Cryer climbed off the wobbly chair and went to peer into Silas's desk. "Are you sure, Silas?"

"You think just because I'm in summer school, I can't keep track of eight lollipops?"

Mrs. Cryer straightened right up. "No. Of course not." She checked around on the floor before announcing, "Class, do we know what happened to Silas's candy?"

No one said anything.

Mrs. Cryer put her hands on her hips. "Okay, whoever has Silas's candy needs to return it right now."

The only thing that happened was the clock ticked louder, the room got hotter, and everyone sat frozen with their uncapped glue sticks drying out.

"Right now," she said, looking us over. "It's important to step up and do the right thing. Stand up and return the candy and that will be the end of it. If the perpetrator comes forward and confesses immediately, there will be no punishment."

Silas crossed his arms and leaned back in his seat. "Yeah, man."

She gave him a look. "It is a reward Silas earned, and whoever has taken them has not only taken the lollipops but has also taken his reward. A reward the perpetrator didn't earn themself."

No one should have been surprised how Mrs. Cryer felt about candy justice. All the same, I wondered if Silas had only lost track of the lollipops. Papa used to say you'd find what you were looking for in the last place you looked. It was a joke. Because after you found what you were looking for, you stopped looking, so of course the missing object was in the last place you checked. Anyway, who was going to sneak over and dig through Silas's desk without anyone noticing? I was too far away—all the way across the room—to see if anyone had been hanging around his desk, but anybody else would have noticed.

Mrs. Cryer rapped her knuckles on Silas's desk. "Who took Silas's candy?"

Everyone looked around at everybody but nobody said anything.

"We all know those lollipops did not grow legs and walk out of this room on their own."

Ivy stuck her hand in the air and started talking at the same time, as though she didn't want us to think her raised hand was a confession. "Maybe he just lost them? Silas? Or he forgot how many he had?"

"No way! I was saving them all for today!"

Madison said how Silas should check his backpack, she found everything in her backpack, and Ivy said she saw Silas eating a lollipop yesterday, and he said he was chewing gum, fool.

Mrs. Cryer stood tall and true in the middle of the room. Still as a statue and just as stony. We were in for it. "Whoever did this needs to step forward right now. I will not dismiss you until that happens. The bell will ring, and we can all sit right here. We can sit here all night. We can sit here all weekend."

The class was dead silent. We never sat so still or so quiet ever in that room. No class had ever sat so still or so quiet in that room.

A long time passed, and it seemed like even longer.

Outside, the idling buses rumbled.

Madison started crying first. She'd been gluing her circle to her caterpillar—it was only her second one, and I didn't know if she hadn't read much or if she was just a slow gluer—and sat frozen, holding her glue stick up, and then wiped her tears on her shoulders.

Cameron's face turned recess red. He had the longest caterpillar in the class and probably got cavities from all the candy he got from Mrs. Cryer. After a while, even Ivy started to cry, and that meant Eddie was at risk, too, staring up at the ceiling, just in case, as if gravity was going to get any tears back into his eyeballs. Eddie couldn't stand to see Ivy cry. I couldn't, either.

Noah took off his glasses and folded the earpieces in and set them on the desk, then pressed his hands right over his eyes. Max put his head down.

But I knew if I believed one lousy thing from Mrs. Cryer, I might have to believe them all. *Low-Low*.

So I didn't believe her.

I refused to believe her.

She couldn't do this. It was against teacher law, or school law, or the regular law.

I wanted to jump up and down and wave my arms and yell, *Come on*. Right? Could a teacher really do this? *Come on*.

Did all these crying kids really believe her? Even if Mrs. Cryer really was not going to let us leave when the bell rang, did these kids believe that not one of their parents would come looking for them? Mine might not—Mom was in the hospital, and Dad was with her or working, and Gram might not realize that I was late—but Ivy's would. Or Eddie's. Or Madison's. Her mom met her every day at the edge of the playground pushing a double stroller loaded with Madison's two little brothers. If a parent didn't start looking, what about the janitor that came by later to sweep up the floor? Didn't they remember that a bus doesn't pull out of the parking lot until it's got a count of kids and then the principal fires up his walkie-talkie and starts sprinting into the building, trying to figure out if the right kid is on the right bus?

But then again, what did I know? Maybe Mrs. Cryer could keep us as long as she wanted. School, after all, was one big, long exercise in all the things I didn't know.

Afternoon announcements came over the loudspeaker. "Bus 78 is bus 15 today. If you normally ride bus 78, today get on bus 15. It's the first bus in line, and Mr. Perry will help direct you."

We started doing what we'd been trained to do at the end of the school day. Madison finally capped her glue stick. Ivy sniffled and stacked up some papers on her desk, and Eddie was halfway to standing.

Mrs. Cryer raised her hand like a crossing guard. "You're dismissed when I say you're dismissed."

Cameron lost it. Put his head down on his desk, his hair sticking up everywhere, his whole back shaking with sobs. Cameron had been in my room since kindergarten. He was all about routine. For the state test, we'd rearranged all the desks into spaced-out rows and sat in alphabetical order, and if Cameron had sat in his usual seat, he probably wouldn't be in summer school right now anyway. Everybody knew this. Even Silas. Who was a turd.

I was mad. I was so mad I could hear buzzing in my head. I held my breath, which is never a good idea, but I knew I was cooking up some anger and I was trying to stop myself. I've been mad before. I know how it can zip through like lightning and how I can do something stupid and hurtful and I'll regret it forever and even though everybody says they love you unconditionally, you kind of wonder why they need to mention it in the first place. So I was holding my breath. Because I knew what it was like. When the mad just gets in the muscles.

"Willow Weaver? Do you have something to say?"

Every head in the room swung toward me. Because I'd stood right up.

"Willow Weaver?"

I felt like a dog with fleas.

Or an anthill filled with ants that gets stomped on the playground and all the ants go running in circles.

A smart kid might have explained how when the bell rang, we all got to go home. We were dismissed. And they would have explained how Mrs. Cryer shouldn't be scaring us like this. But I wasn't a smart kid and so I said something else entirely. I said, "I did it. I took the candy."

The class gasped in one big hiss. I heard one kid say they knew it, they knew I did it, but I couldn't figure out who, and

Mrs. Cryer told them to hush. Silas didn't even bother looking triumphant and sat with his arms crossed. When I spoke, he whipped his gaze down to his feet. Madison's eyes were stuck on me, her mouth hanging open, and Cameron still had his head down on his desk, still crying.

Mrs. Cryer gestured to Silas as though all of a sudden she was a graceful ballerina. "Return it to Silas now, please."

Silas said, "Nah. I don't want it anymore," and for the first time Mrs. Cryer looked mad. "Cooties," he added by way of an explanation. Mrs. Cryer gave that big, aggrieved sigh that was usually just for me.

"Good. Because I ate them." That wasn't true at all. It was a big fat lie. "I ate them," I repeated, big and loud. "I ate them all."

Which was stupid. If anyone was really paying attention they'd know it was a lie. Because if I'd sat there that afternoon and chomped my way through a pile of lollipops, someone would have noticed. Even if they were the tiny ones. Even if teachers thought we were the kind of kids who didn't pay attention, we would have noticed, because the trouble is we're really the kind of kids who are paying attention to every last single thing.

The dismissal bell sounded. It was loud. Everyone grabbed their stuff and busted out of there.

Chapter 12

The last time I buzzed with that kind of anger was right after Papa's funeral and we were back at Gram and Papa's house, though now it was only Gram's.

Gram has a hutch that sits in the space between the living room and the kitchen. It's mostly filled with china she never used. She said she'd have to wash it by hand if she did, and then she'd usually say she didn't know why she bothered having dishes like that in the first place. I said we could use it whenever. If she wanted. Mom volunteered to wash it and said I could dry, and Gram said, "Oh, I don't know if I'd trust it to a kid." Gram didn't want a solution. She was just complaining. When Gram got like that Mom called it venting. I'm only allowed to vent in my room by myself with the door closed. We always had to listen to Gram, though. Because she's old, listening to her vent is being respectful.

After Papa's funeral and burial, church ladies set out a lunch for us in the dark and stuffy church basement. There was a row of slow cookers filled with meats for sandwiches and mini hot dogs in sauce. Mom looked sick to her stomach and I didn't know if it was because some of the food looked like canned dog food, or because of sadness, or the baby (which right then was a secret), or all of the above. The church ladies had sad smiles for us and quietly set out new piles of paper napkins and poured weak lemonade and told us which cups were lemonade and which were water because no one could tell but no one really cared, anyway.

One of the ladies came back to Gram's house to help, after. She didn't know about the china plates.

She pulled them out of the hutch even though there were paper plates on the table right next to her and didn't know that the reason she had to pull on the door so hard was because no one ever opened it. Mom let her. Gram had already gone back to her bedroom and closed the door. Gram hadn't even taken off her shoes or put down her purse.

It was just me, Mom, the church lady, some of Papa's old cousins, and Dad.

The nice church lady put some store-bought shortbread cookies on a china plate and arranged them into rows of semicircles.

The white plate with the tiny and delicate blue flowers. Antique. They were antiques even to Gram. They'd been Papa's grandmother's.

I didn't know that. Not until after.

Hank was stretched out right under the table, near the church lady's feet. Under the table was one of his favorite places to sleep. Papa always said it showed how smart Hank was. How he liked to sleep there. No one would step on him. He was safe and out of view and protected from careless human feet. The church lady's shoes were navy blue with short heels that weren't any higher than a wad of chewing gum. They were the most boring-looking shoes in the world, but I guess they smelled interesting. No one told her to take them off, and she hadn't asked, and Hank woke up and started sniffing her shoes. Then he sniffed around the church lady's skirt, lifted his nose to sniff the food, then stuck his nose back down between his front paws and whinnied softly. He was sad.

The church lady said, "Oh, goodness, I didn't know you had a dog there!"

I said too loudly because I was surprised, "You didn't know we had a dog? Everybody knows my grandpa has dogs."

"Is that right?" She smiled her sad, weak lemonade smile and set out more cookies on the antique heirloom china plate.

It was like lightning, how it happened so fast, how that burn in my stomach zapped up through my muscles and made me pick up the china plate with its shortbread cookies before I even knew what I was doing. It was a dangerous feeling. A feeling like that can make you hurl a china plate at the sliding back door and send cookies flying everywhere and turn the plate to smithereens and make Hank lose his ever-loving mind. Before you know it, a feeling like that can get the church lady to let Hank out the front door because maybe Hank got zapped by that same burning feeling of anger and sadness together, and Hank actually bolts out the front door like it's the worst kind of miracle.

I chased after him.

I wore black pants I had just about outgrown and they were tight on my calves and ended on the wrong side of my ankles, and shoes that pinched my feet. My black sweater was new. Dad had had to go out and buy it the night before because

I didn't have anything right for a funeral and Mom said she wasn't worried but then Gram said she hoped I'd be proper, and so Dad drove nearly an hour to the Walmart and bought the only thing they had, which was black but sparkly, and Dad and I had cut the sequins off it that morning. I saved them. The sweater had been pretty, before. I wanted to sew them back on but I knew I never would, because it would always be a funeral sweater and now it was the *I did this* sweater.

Hank ran like it was a race, like he had somewhere to go, like it was a getaway. Like the only way to get out of the house was to go like a rocket. He ran as though he was never going to get tired. I thought maybe this was a good thing. Maybe now he could go through doorways.

But it was just a terrified dog running in circles around the house and the outside of the surrounding fence, and me chasing him. I opened up both gates—one on the side and one near the garage—hoping Hank would know that he could go on through, but he just kept running.

Eddie came panting up beside me. He lived a few backyards over and behind Gram's. He was still in his funeral clothes, too, stiff dark jeans, a black button-down shirt, and a tie.

Eddie chased after Hank and I stood by the gate, and when Eddie got Hank close, he about sat on him and pushed him through the gate, as though poor Hank was some kind of bucking bronco. I latched the gate closed, ran to close the other gate, and Eddie climbed up and over the rattling fence. The three of us all stood around panting: Hank in the yard,

Eddie bent over with his hands on his knees, and me leaning against the fence.

"That's like a miracle, right?" Eddie asked between pants. "That he just went out the door?"

"Maybe. Could be."

But it wasn't. It wasn't a miracle. It was a scared and freaked-out dog.

Later, Dad and I washed all the dishes. We dried the plates and stacked them all back in the hutch. The nice church lady had swept up all the broken china and then vacuumed and then she left. I felt awful. All over, everywhere, and for every reason. Dad was just business. When I said something about it, he said, "Later, okay?"

Mom had gone back to Gram's room and was sleeping next to her on the bed. Everyone else had gone home. Hank was still in the backyard, lying with his snout between his paws, but he wasn't a problem yet. Dad watched the weather report, over and over again, and I stood at the sliding kitchen door looking outside until Dad started paying attention and told me that even though the floor had been cleaned, I shouldn't stand there with my bare feet.

We walked home, after, me and Mom and Dad. It was spring and everything smelled like mud. Mom said, "I can't believe you did that, Lolo. What were you thinking?" Then she held up a hand to stop me from answering because she didn't really want to know what I was thinking, which is something that happens if you're a kid and you've done something like smash a plate not by accident against a door after your grandfather's funeral. "Don't say anything. Jeez. Do you think we needed a temper tantrum on top of anything else? You didn't even behave like that when you were a toddler. I'm not going to have two babies around here, am I?"

That was the night Hank started howling.

When I was brave 2
—Noah

There was a guy named Pavlov who trained his dogs to think food was being served every time he rang a bell, and so every time he rang a bell the dogs salivated and looked for their food. My mom says she salivates whenever she smells popcorn. I know what makes every kid in summer school salivate in July when it is 99.99 degrees outside, and it is the dismissal bell.

My mom says kids and dogs are not the same and I should cool my jets.

I don't know if what the girl who sits by the pencil sharpener did was brave or not, but it was something, that's for sure. I wish I had done something other than sit and get stressed out. I wish I had stood up and said, "I've got a bus to catch!" Because you can't do stuff like that, Mrs. Cryer, and say that you can keep us at school forever until someone confesses. What if someone really believed you? Because there was no way you could have been telling the truth. Right?

Chapter 13

First thing after we got out of summer school that day, Ivy told me how she knew I didn't really take the candy. "Right, Lo?"

Eddie told me not to worry. No way would I get in trouble. I asked him why not, since Mrs. Cryer liked to cause me trouble.

"Because she'd have to admit to it," he said. Eddie shook his head. "Saying she'd never let us go home. She can't do that. All the parents would be so mad."

"Everybody believed her," I said. He'd believed her, too.

Ivy kicked at a chunk of crumbling blacktop as we walked by the Frozen Fish. Its parking lot and seating area were starting to look as sad as the rest of the lake. "I believed her," she said. Her face was still flushed pink from crying.

Instead of going to the empty all-beach beach, we went to the dollar store.

The dollar store smells like flip-flops, but it's not the summer kind of flip-flops in the backyard smell, it's a stinky and cheap kind of smell. Gram always says how it smells like a tire dump. We wandered through the dog toy section and Eddie squeaked every squeaky toy there. I picked out a pair of hot-pink sunglasses and Ivy tried on some white ones with fake rhinestones, and then I finally made it over to the candy aisle.

Ivy, behind her white rhinestone sunglasses, asked me

about it. "You're getting lollipops? I'd think you'd never want to see another lollipop again in your life."

"Mrs. Cryer said that for everything to be forgotten the thief had to return the reward candy."

"Wait," Ivy said. "So you did take them?"

"Of course not." I huffed out a breath. "I only said I did."

"Oh." She snapped some of the hair bands she wore around her wrist. "But why?"

"Why? I just couldn't stand it, that's why. I couldn't stand it so much it just sort of happened. Me saying that. So we could all go home. I wanted it to be over. I mean, you said you believed her, Ivy."

We were the only customers and there was no line for checkout, not without tourists buying snacks or beach toys. Ivy and I bought our sunglasses and I bought the lollipops, even though I didn't want to spend any stupid money on stupid Silas. Sometimes things at the dollar store can cost more than a dollar, and these were three for a dollar, so I ended up with nine, and I hated giving him one more but Ivy was right. I didn't really want to even think about lollipops. I gave the extra to Ivy because no way was I giving Silas one more than I had to. Eddie bought a squeaky rubber chicken. The tag said it was a dog toy, but the way Eddie was messing with it, Ivy said it was more like an Eddie toy.

***

Monday morning at school I gave the eight dollar-store lollipops to Mrs. Cryer, who didn't say anything but gave them to

Silas, who shoved them into his backpack. I sat at my faraway desk and watched the sink drip because it always dripped. I'd waited all weekend for Mrs. Cryer or the principal to call Gram, or to hear from Dad that he'd had a call, but nothing. I'm a pest, but I've never gotten into big trouble. I never threw a punch on the playground or chucked food in the cafeteria, or shoved anyone, or wandered the halls when I said I was going to the bathroom. I was just a pain in the neck. So I didn't know exactly what it was like to get into real trouble, but that Monday morning still nothing happened. Maybe Mrs. Cryer meant it when she said that if the thief owned up, they wouldn't get in trouble. Or maybe Eddie was right when he said how Mrs. Cryer couldn't get me in trouble because then she'd also be in trouble.

The only thing that did happen that Monday was that Mrs. Cryer looked right at me when she read our journal prompt aloud.

"If you had a time machine, where in time would you travel?"

I knew what she wanted.

She wanted a nice long journal entry about me going back in time and maybe not taking Silas's reading-reward candy. Except I didn't take Silas's candy, so I couldn't write about that. Maybe I was supposed to go back in time and guard his desk. Or maybe I was supposed to see who had really taken it. No way. And I wasn't even going to go back to the last seven minutes of that afternoon when I'd given a false confession, because I didn't even regret that, and I didn't think that was allowed. I mean, everyone knows you can't go back in time and change things, no matter how much you want to. Didn't Mrs. Cryer even know the rules of time travel?

In my journal I drew a hard, heavy line, top to bottom, down the middle of the page. I'd pressed too hard on the pencil, and the line looked as angry as I felt. It marked the other pages behind it in the notebook, and I was sorry about it.

Have you ever been in a moment, and you know, you know down into your bones, that from that moment forward, nothing will ever be the same? Maybe if your parents say they're getting divorced, or if school shuts down for months, or if the governor says a mud tsunami could wipe out your entire town in twenty minutes, or if someone dies. It's so big and monumental, it's a mark on your timeline. It's a destination for your time machine. Every ordinary day after is strange and unbelievable.

I almost got started on what I wanted to say. I almost wrote *Papa*, but then I got stuck, because of *is* and *was*.

Is is now, and *was* is past, gone, behind you, and I don't think it makes any sense. Why was I supposed to say Papa *was* my grandfather? He's gone, but he's still my grandfather. That's a fact. How could it change? Mom, Gram, Dad, Michelle the dog lady, they all catch themselves and change their *is*s to *was*s, but not me. That's the kind of mistake I'm not ever going to want to fix.

Thinking about making mistakes made me think about Chickpea Garbanzo.

A big sister is supposed to be a good example. Smart. Good grades. No summer school. Good with dogs. Helpful. No temper tantrums. Brave.

When I thought about the little baby, curled up and not much bigger than a butternut squash, I thought about how helpless a baby was and how I mostly knew about dogs and, even then, what I knew about dogs wasn't much.

Dad told me that I could teach the baby—when he or she was a lot bigger than a butternut squash—all the things Papa taught me, but it wasn't really helpful advice.

Mom had said I didn't have to be a good example, and I'd asked, stunned, What do you mean? Don't you think I can be a good example? I mean, I'd traumatized a traumatized dog. I back talked. I lied. Was Mom thinking about all that? But Mom said all I have to do is love the baby. She said, "If you just love him or her, the rest is going to fall into place. Just be a good person. Good people do good things. A good person will be a good sister."

That helped. A little. But that baby is going to be a whole new person who will never know Papa. Papa being gone is a whole new heavy line right down the middle of a sheet of paper that no one can cross over.

The baby was going to be born on the other side of that line.

It was a whole new step into a future without Papa.

And a time machine wouldn't fix it.

*If you had a time machine, where in time would
you travel?*

—Noah

*If I had a time machine I'd travel back in time to see the
first moment when a wolf emerges from the forest (maybe)
to sit at a human's campfire and watch a human feed the wolf
scraps of (woolly mammoth? saber-toothed tiger?) meat. Or
maybe that human would be me, even though a time trav-
eler isn't supposed to interfere. I'd be the ancient human kid
who turned the feral wolf tame and tamed those wolf's pups
and then the grandpups, and that's how we have dogs as pets
today. And if I'm not the kid, then I'm the first witness. I see
the moment when wolves made human contact and began
to be pets, and if it's not a wolf with a kid and meat scraps,
whatever it is, I'm there. When I return to the present time,
I'll finally know something other people don't. I can say the
truth. I can say, "Here's exactly what happened. I know." If
it's different from how people think it is, I can say, "That's
not how it happened! I know! I was there!"*

Chapter 14

I thought and thought about it. I thought about it during test practice when I was filling the answer bubbles all the way in. I thought about it at recess, which was mostly trying to find shade under the skinny trees that edge the playground and watching kids play basketball. I thought about it at Gram's when we had sliced (farmers' market) tomatoes with olive oil, salt, and basil, and then BLT sandwiches, and when Gram told me not to slouch at the table. I thought about it when I spoke with my mom on the phone, who sounded exactly the same as always, and we didn't talk about the baby, the future, or being a good example. I thought about it at night in the guest room at Gram's while her flowery curtains fluttered in the breeze from the open window and the dark shapes of her little wooden sheep looked strange and lonely, and I thought about it when I only heard crickets outside and no dogs barking.

It didn't matter.

I already knew the answer.

I already had the solution.

If I got Hank back, the baby who could never know Papa could know Hank, at least a little. If I got Hank back, Gram would have some of Papa back, too, more than a closet full of his clothes and his shoes lined up in the garage, more than his dog-fur-coated pickup truck that she didn't want to drive but didn't want to sell, more than the container of cottage cheese I'd found in the fridge, its expiration date from back when Papa was alive. Gram could love Hank and Hank could love Gram, and I could love Hank, because I did, and it was my fault and I'd made it so he had to go.

***

I told Ivy and Eddie how I was going to get Hank back when we were walking home from school. How I was going to go out across the lake in Papa's yellow canoe and get Hank and bring him home, forever.

Eddie was stalking after the geese, pulling his arms up like a big bird with broken wings trying to take off. Ivy got distracted and yelled at him about how he was going to get attacked. We saw it once, walking home from school. How a goose chased a kid—a high schooler, who tried to act cool but then flat-out ran. The goose flew up and stuck out its neck like it was some sort of black snake and snapped at the kid's backside and knocked him right onto the sidewalk in front of the dollar store. The goose skimmed over him, kind of flying, kind of running, and then escaped out to the lake, back when we had water.

Ivy and I followed Eddie. We stood on the dam and I told them what I was going to do. The dam looked just like grass and ground until you were right at the edge, but on the lake side the wall looked like a wall. In most places there wasn't a beach or slope to get into the water, it was just going to be one big jump.

These days, the lake was a scummy and scuzzy half-drained bathtub. Water weeds poked up through the water, and land weeds were popping up in the mud and spreading to where the water started. Gram said she heard that there were pumpkin plants sprouting near the public beach, and some people said that if the lake never went back to the way it was, it could be turned into the world's biggest pumpkin patch, and then I imagined someone in the future wondering why on earth the lakeless town was called Sycamore Lake and why the pumpkin patch was called Sycamore Lake Swampy Pumpkins. Or something like that.

I tried standing like the Statue of Liberty, with my arm in the air holding an imaginary torch, and announced, "I'm going to get Hank back."

Eddie asked, "How are you going to do that?"

"With a canoe. I'm going to take my grandfather's canoe out, get Hank, and bring him back to Gram."

Ivy turned to me and did that thing where she thinks she's raising one eyebrow but she's actually just squinting. "Seriously?"

"Gram needs Hank back. It was a mistake to ever let him go. I'm going to fix it."

Ivy asked, "How do you even know where he is? And I mean, is he even at a place with boat access? Is he really that close?"

"My mom told me where Hank is across the lake. I looked it up on satellite maps. I know where I'm going. It's just across the lake and then across the street, across the state route."

"Whoa," Ivy said, and Eddie said, "Yeah, watch out for the semitrucks."

We all three looked at where the lake used to be. Eddie nodded once, serious. He was there after the plate throwing. He understood about how and why Hank was gone. He knew how I was responsible. "When are you heading out?"

"Has to be tomorrow," I answered. Tomorrow was Friday, and we didn't have summer school on Fridays.

Ivy asked, "Don't you need to practice paddling the canoe? Maybe you should wait."

"Nah," I answered. "It's like riding a bike. Plus the Fourth of July is coming up."

Eddie snapped into his Statue of Liberty pose. "Bet that's why Mrs. Cryer was extra grumpy about the lollipops. No boat parade."

"I know there's no big celebration this year for Independence Day," I said, "but you just never can tell. People like any excuse to set off fireworks."

Ivy still squinted at me. "Your gram actually said it was okay?"

"I'll say I'm with you, okay, Ivy? I mean, she might even think I'm in school. It won't take more than a few hours." I looked it up. A slow canoer can canoe at about two miles an hour and the lake was seven miles long and about a quarter mile across, except at the wide spot, which was where I was going to go. Straight across. Mostly. Maybe I'd have to go a little farther on the long end of the lake. I wasn't sure. Some of my teachers might be surprised to know that I can do the math but I figured maybe the trip would be a couple hours out and a couple hours back. No boats with motors had been on the lake since it had been drained by the Army Core of Engineers. Fishing was allowed, but I never saw anybody out there. And soon most of the shore would be fenced off for construction, so how would anybody get a boat out, anyway? No one would notice me. The lake used to be the center of the world, but no one looked at the lake anymore. Who wanted to look at it? Nobody, that's who.

Why don't teachers ever ask students to write about that?

What's gone? What's the worst thing you've ever done? How will you fix it? If you had a canoe, where would you go? What if you had a canoe but had no lake to put it in?

Ivy asked, "You got a life jacket?"

"Yeah."

She asked, "Do you have *two*? One for the dog?"

"Of course I do." I was insulted she would even ask. Of course Papa had them, hanging up in the garage next to the people life jackets. "Anyway," I went on, "who's going to drown in that puddle of a lake out there?"

Ivy pointed a finger at me. "A person can drown in a bucket!"

"Debris is probably your biggest problem," Eddie warned. "Tossed off coolers and tires and boat pieces."

Ivy asked, "Are you sure you want to be out on that water? It's pretty yucky these days."

"Yeah," agreed Eddie. "Don't forget the goose poop. It's all, you know, concentrated now. Industrial strength."

"It's just shallow," I told them. "That will make it safer, don't you think? Anyway, it's not like that other lake that no one's been allowed to swim in for, like, ten years." The other lake was about three hours away and across the state. When newspapers wrote about our lake, they always wrote about that other one, too. Hard rains happened more and more, washing more and more fertilizer off the surrounding farm fields into the lake, and the lake water was warmer than it ever was before, making it a great big stew to grow algae. It also happened up on Lake Erie—the rising water temperatures and all the washed-off nitrogen from fertilizers even made it so that once an entire city was told they couldn't drink their tap water for three whole days. "Our lake is only in trouble because of the dams, right?" Ivy and Eddie didn't answer. "It's not like I'm *swimming* across. And Hank's an experienced canoe dog."

Ivy said, "Maybe we could find someone to give you a ride."

"Who?"

"A taxi cab?" Eddie offered. "Or a ride app?"

"That would cost a fortune in allowance," Ivy said.

"The canoe is the best way," I said. "And if Gram asks, remember that I'm with you all day Friday. And Saturday, too."

Ivy's jaw dropped. "Lolo. If you're not back by Friday night, your grandmother will call the police. *I'll* call the police. *Eddie* will call the police."

"I'm just planning ahead. It's not going to take that long. You know it isn't."

Eddie said it was a sure thing how I'd be back before dark. He told me, "You've got to wear a hat out on the water. Do you have a hat?"

"Somewhere."

Eddie swiped his ball cap off his head and stuck it on mine. It was dark green. Camo. The brim was perfectly rounded and it smelled sweaty and also like the hot school blacktop and freshly cut grass. Without his hat, Eddie blinked against the bright sunlight like a nocturnal animal out at the wrong time. His hair was matted down and then it curled up at the very edges, because he always wore that hat. Ivy bumped shoulders with him, doing that cousin thing.

"Thanks, Eddie," I said, settling the hat down snuggly on my head. "Are you sure?"

He ruffled his dark hair. "I'm sure." He smiled.

I wondered if he meant it.

Eddie said, "You got this."

I wasn't sure if he was telling the truth or if he really believed it, but Eddie had a way of saying things that made me believe it. *You got this.*

"Yeah," Ivy chimed in. "You've got this."

Chapter 15

Is it sneaking in if it's your house? And it's just that you're not supposed to be there? I mean, I have a key, after all. I went over right after I went my way and Eddie and Ivy went theirs, and tiptoed around, gathering what I needed. The house was closed up and stuffy. No one had opened windows or run the AC in a while. Dirty dishes sat in the sink, and I thought about washing them. It's the kind of thing Gram would have done, before. Bustle on over and wash the dishes and put a casserole in the fridge and collect the mail and then volunteer Papa to mow the lawn. So I washed the dishes. It's not my favorite thing. It was also a two-part tactical error. One, because if anybody ever thought I had enough gumption to clean up after a mess without being told, they'd think it was something I could do all the time. And two, because it used up too much of my time and it took me longer to find the sunscreen and gather up some snacks.

I was digging around under my parents' bathroom sink looking for the waterproof sunscreen when I heard the sounds of someone in the house who wasn't trying to be sneaky about it.

Dad.

His boots thunked on the floor as he toed them off, and his big key ring with all the rental keys jingled as he hung it on the hook by the door.

I stepped into the hallway with the sunscreen. "Dad?"

"What are you doing here, Lo?"

I held up the sunscreen. "I needed some stuff."

"You should be at your grandmother's." He looked tired. He needed a shave, and his hair was matted down. His shirt was sweat stained. I didn't get close enough to tell, but I'd bet he also didn't smell good.

"I just stopped by."

"Does she know you're here? Your gram?"

"Probably not. I stopped by on my way home from school."

He nodded and poured a big glass of water and then dug in the freezer for some microwave food. If he noticed anything about the clean dishes, he didn't say so. Even though it should have been good news, I was disappointed.

"How's Mom? Can you take me over tonight?"

"Sorry, Lo," he answered, ripping open the microwave dinner box. I knew he meant it. He was sorry. "I've got a few hours before my shift at the warehouse and I won't be heading to the hospital till after. I'm trying to stay the night there." Dad had told me how the room had an uncomfortable bench that turned into an uncomfortable bed. He said his feet hung off the edge. "I know your mom would sure like your company, though. Your gram will take you."

I shook my head. "You know how she feels about city traffic. And city parking lots. And parking garages. And, you know. How she feels about just doing stuff."

He said what Mom always said. "Your gram is tough as nails."

"I don't know about that, Dad."

Dad smiled and said, as if he believed it, "You can talk her into it. You're pretty tenacious once you set your mind to something. Tell her she doesn't even have to take the highway. She can take 16 all the way in, right to the hospital."

I liked that Dad called me tenacious, but I still didn't think there was any talking Gram into a trip, even if Gram knew all the different roads to take. She had them all in her head. She didn't even use an app or a GPS. She'd lived here forever, and she knew where things were. She'd just get huffy if I told her what route Dad said she should take. She'd say something like, *As if there won't be traffic on those roads, too.*

"Maybe I can take you tomorrow afternoon? I've got some time then."

"Maybe not tomorrow," I said. I had plans.

A mistake you made
—Noah

When my brother kept making mistakes and spelling his name wrong, everybody thought it was cute. His name is Brian but he always spelled it Brain *and everyone thought that was funny and now mostly people call him The Brain, like that mistake just proved how smart he is. He gets smart kid toys for presents, like robot-building kits. When I make a mistake, I end up in summer school and nobody thinks it's cute. Nobody's ever given me a robot kit. Mom says that's because they're expensive. If I started spelling my name wrong somebody would take me to a doctor. When I spelled words wrong on a spelling test Mom would make me write the words out, over and over, and Dad would quiz me in the car on the drive to school, and later Mom would tell him that's not how I learn, I need to write it out, and Dad would say, "What? You want him jabbing a pencil around in the back seat? You want him to poke out his eye?" They bicker a lot like that. They can't have a conversation without a side of bickering. They're divorced. It's not that bad.*

Chapter 16

The canoe weighs twelve pounds, which Eddie said was how much he weighed when he was born. Twelve pounds is a lot for a baby, I guess, but not much for a canoe.

I carried the yellow canoe on my shoulder and held it in place with one hand and carried the paddle with the other. While the canoe wasn't heavy, it was long. That was the only tricky thing about it. But all I needed to do was cross the empty street and get it out to the water.

I had my backpack, two life jackets, food sealed up in plastic bags, water, a foldable doggy water bowl, the hot-pink sunglasses from the dollar store, sunscreen, and Eddie's hat.

I took small steps across the wet grass. It had rained that morning and I had to wait until nearly lunchtime when the weather radar showed it clearing. It was sunny now and steamy and the perfect day to jump in the lake (all summer days were perfect days to jump in the lake), if we'd still had a real one. Gram was surprised when I told her that there was no summer school on Fridays, and I wished it hadn't rained because it would have been so easy to act as though it was a school day. But it's not as though I wanted to go hide out in the garage. So after the rain cleared I just told her how I was going to Ivy's, and Gram said okay, said maybe she'd call my mom later, maybe we'd go visit soon, and she settled in to her cooking shows, spaced-out, and I thought about how happy she'd be to have Hank back again. It wouldn't be like having Papa back, but maybe it was the next best thing.

I climbed down over the edge of the dam and went out over rocks and mud to meet the water.

It was all gray and quiet. Not too far away, a flock of geese had spread out but for once they weren't interested in me.

I pretended I knew exactly what I was doing and knew exactly how to do it.

Sometimes the weeds caught the paddle and I had to tug it free. Sometimes the water was so low the canoe scraped against the bottom of the lake or the paddle hit it. Tall grasses brushed against the canoe. I couldn't believe this was ever a pretty vacation place with tourists and boats. I couldn't believe I ever went swimming here. It was a whole different place than it used to be.

When I looked back to the road and the town I couldn't see anything, only the small hill that was the edge of the lake. That was because I was down so low. It was probably a good thing, to be hidden from view. Normally, on higher water and in a boat, I'd be able to see Gram's house, the village, and the crowd of people and seagulls at the Frozen Fish.

A dragonfly skittered over the water and flew by my face. The water was a bug paradise. Gnats glommed onto the water along with water bugs. Flies buzzed at my ears.

I tried to think of the right words about how it felt to be in the canoe as it moved through the water in the after-rain sun, with its own special light, and have this whole part of the world to myself, even if it was stinky and swampy. Not that I'd ever write them down for anybody to read, but so that I could remember. It all made me think of Papa. In my heart, as sure as anything, my memory of Papa was so strong I didn't even want to turn my head to look around in case I saw him. Or in case I didn't. Did Gram or Mom ever feel that way?

It took me a while to get my rhythm. Dip to the right, dip to the left. Like squeezing toothpaste out of the tube, Papa would say. Easy. Anybody could do it. Even me. I could do it.

It never was a very clear lake. It was muddy and always churned up by boats, so I could never see down to the bottom, and I couldn't now. The water was dark and greenish with plants. I didn't see any pumpkins.

Orange construction fencing had gone up in some places. There were orange construction barrels and signs, too far away to read, and some pieces of heavy equipment around. Past that was a section of the lake with bigger and older houses. They weren't crammed in the way they were in the village, all those little vacation places squeezed up together. Weeping willow trees stood near the shore, their branches falling toward the water. There was a giant old sycamore tree, too, with a big, low, and crooked branch that ran along the shoreline. In a real summer, it looked like a good place to climb and then jump into the water.

Out of nowhere, someone started shouting. "Excuse me! Excuse me! Hello!"

Behind the willow and the sycamore was an old house. It

was big and white. A green lawn sloped down to the edge of the lake. A white gazebo sat in the middle of the lawn. It was one of the biggest and fanciest houses on the lake, and probably one of the oldest, too. Maybe it had even sat there before Sycamore Lake was a lake and just a low wetland.

A woman in a large, floppy sun hat stood at the edge of a long dock that hadn't been removed yet. She called out again. "You there!"

She looked suspended in midair. Just stuck out in the sky, on the way to nowhere. No land to step foot on and the water far, far below. She stuck her arm out at me and yelled. "You!"

I didn't recognize her at first. Not far away up on the dock. Not in the floppy hat. She knew me, though. She hollered, "Willow Weaver! Are you wearing a life jacket?"

How had she known it was me? What kind of cruel teacher trick was that? It was just my own dumb luck that in the life jacket, Eddie's baseball cap, and in Papa's canoe, the worst teacher in the world would recognize me.

I thought about paddling away. I mean, what would she do? Jump in and follow me?

"Where is your life jacket!" It was a question, but Mrs. Cryer was clearly working on using all her lung power.

I aimed the paddle straight at her and grabbed the front of the vest where it buckled across my chest, wondering if she needed her vision checked. "This *is* a life jacket!"

"Don't get smart with me, young lady. There is no call to get fresh when someone is concerned for your safety."

She wasn't in charge of me today. Not on a Friday. Not outside her classroom. She should have forgotten all about me. At least for the weekend. You'd think she'd want to.

Mrs. Cryer bent up the brim of her hat. "The lake is closed."

"For motor boats," I said. "And swimming. Fishing's allowed."

She stuck her hands on her hips. "And are you fishing?" She looked pink and sweaty, like the inside of a sorry winter grocery-store tomato. "It doesn't look like it to me. Where are you going?"

Even though I could just paddle away, the training to answer a teacher is strong, so I told her. "Up the lake. And then back."

You'd think she'd like that. She'd already told us how we should be playing outside and riding bikes and not inside playing video games.

She harrumphed from the dock. "Well, then. Safe travels. Keep your life jacket on."

"Sure thing." It felt good to paddle away, even if I had to tug the paddle out of a knot of weeds.

Then Mrs. Cryer shouted out, "Isn't this just like you, Willow Weaver!"

Mrs. Cryer meant rude, reckless, careless, trouble.

She didn't mean brave.

Chapter 17

After Mrs. Cryer's place, the lake was less familiar.

The canoe was like a cup that gathered heat and sunshine. I was sweaty. Hot. My skin had that shrinking feeling from the sun. I thought about walking, in the sludge, in the weeds, towing the canoe, but I figured that would be just as much work, even if I'd be wet, which would be good.

Sycamore Lake isn't actually a very big lake, but all lakes are big when you're out in the middle of them.

I drifted past the closed Burger Bar. Its windows were dark and the patio umbrellas were closed and covered with white splotches, courtesy of the gulls that liked to hang around.

The water petered out before the shore, and I ran the canoe aground in muck and rocks and weeds that slipped across my ankles like grasping hands. I left the canoe and my gear at the edge of the lake, alongside a dock that had been pulled ashore. I knew I wouldn't be able to get the canoe, paddle, and Hank across the busy road, so it was just me, my pack, and Eddie's ball cap as I snuck through yards filled with leftover summer vacations: covered boats, boat trailers, dock pieces, grills on decks, faded garden flags. No people. No lawn chairs. No drying beach towels. Rows of narrow lake houses stood between me and the road. There was no one around. There weren't even cars parked in the driveways. It didn't matter that it was a summer Friday. No one was coming to visit a smelly lake they couldn't swim in and couldn't boat in and couldn't zoom across for pizza.

Across the country road with double yellow lines and a road-kill speed limit was the house. Old. Gray. The grass was patchy and weedy. The barn was gray, too, and its big doors were open and showed only darkness. There was a basketball hoop but the rim was bent down in a way that meant no one could ever shoot a basket. All the house's windows were open, which was a sure sign the old place didn't have air-conditioning. Most of the houses around the lake were pretty new but not this one. If it had been right on the lake, someone would have bought it and torn it down and put up condos.

It was easy-peasy lemon squeezy. Eddie was right. *You got this.* For once, something felt good, and for once I was really getting it done.

A long dog run stretched from the corner of the barn and out behind the house, which was pretty much an open yard filled with dandelions. The house didn't have a fenced-in yard and if there was an invisible fence I'd buy Silas more lollipops.

You got this.

The sounds went from insects whirring to excited dog yips. Hank.

Hank ran toward me, the line of his dog run clacking. He jumped, happy, and the leash pulled on his neck, and I didn't like that. I wanted to get him home to Gram's big open yard. Still, he barked happily and wagged his tail so hard it thwapped my legs and I thought we'd both fall over. He licked my hands and sniffed me and my life jacket and Eddie's hat. I whispered how he was coming home with me, and we were going to help Gram, and I was sorry, though I left out all the things about plates and doorways. I was so glad to see Hank my heart was about to burst. It was the kind of feeling I hadn't had in a long time.

Just as I was about to unclip him from the run, a door slammed as loud as a backfiring pickup truck.

I knew right away by the way the door slammed that it was a kid who was coming for me.

"Stop! Stop! That's my dog!"

Chapter 18

It was Noah.

Noah from summer school.

Noah with the dark, sturdy glasses.

Noah, who wrote so much in his journal he'd worn down at least two pencils to stubs at the sharpener next to my exile desk and Mrs. Cryer told him he could take his notebook home if he needed to, but right now he needed to *Close it, please*, and *Switch gears*.

Noah, who had my dog.

Those were his big open barn doors that were supposed to be healing to Hank.

In one great leap, Noah landed on Hank and threw his arms around him and pushed me, but I held on.

You know how a dog crouches and snarls and shows its teeth? That was me, inside, and I figured Noah and I had the same look, and we were both the human equivalent of a crouched and snarling dog. I was nothing but angry and snapping teeth.

Noah found words that weren't snarls first. "This is my dog," he said.

I was so deep into dog and feelings it took me a while to find any words that weren't me growling right back. Finally I got out, "Hank's not your dog and he's coming with me."

"You're a kidnapper."

I dug my fingers tighter around Hank's collar. "Hank's not a kid."

"You're a dognapper."

"Hank is my grandfather's dog and we need him back. My grandmother can't live without him. We love him."

Noah said, "I know what you are, Willow Weaver."

"Lolo."

"You took those lollipops and now you're stealing my dog."

"I only said I took those lollipops because everybody was crying and I wanted to get us out of there."

"Right."

The way he'd decided I was already a thief made it easy for me not to give up on getting Hank back.

Noah tightened his arms around Hank. He tried to grab the collar, too, but my hands were there and there wasn't any room, not without hurting Hank, and neither one of us was going to do that.

"Hank's your foster dog," I said. "He's not actually yours."

"Not yet."

We were so close it was all hot, panting dog breath, and the two of us, talking right at each other.

Noah looked at me as though maybe I was feral. Maybe he was right. "I know who your grandmother is," he said. "Your grandmother gave Hank away."

"She didn't mean it."

"I kind of think she did," he said.

"It was a mistake. We need Hank back. And we had him first."

"We're fostering Hank now. No givebacks."

I didn't say anything about how I loved Hank, or how it was my fault that Hank had to be rehomed in the first place. Noah Pham wouldn't care about that. I knew that. I knew that before he'd brought up the missing reading-reward candy. So I told him how everything was wrong at his house. How a big fenced yard was better than a run on a high-speed roadkill road and how dogs slipped out of their collars all the time. How my grandfather was pretty much a dog whisperer. How Gram needed company and someone to take care of. "And it's too hot out here," I said, nearly out of breath by then. "Is there ever any shade? Does he even go into that barn? Even if he does, that's not a *real* home for him. A barn. Away from people." Noah didn't answer, so I kept going. "It's no good. Only the worst kind of person won't take care of a dog. You've got to always do right by a dog."

Noah looked heartbroken but I couldn't stop. It was like riding a bike downhill. Too dangerous to stop suddenly.

I said, "Hank needs to be with his people. We know how to take care of a dog like Hank. We're the ones who really love him. I'm taking Hank home with me. You haven't had Hank for very long at all. We had Hank for months. Hank knows us. We're his home."

A semitruck rumbled as it sped past the house on the two-lane road, proving my point.

When Noah spoke, it was so soft I could hardly hear him. "Okay." He started crying, though I could tell he was trying not to. He stuck his face right into Hank's fur and Hank wiggled around to lick his cheek. "Okay. If it's best for Hank. You know he's a special dog, right?"

I nodded. I knew. "I know all about Hank. I promise."

"Okay." He hugged Hank for a while longer and stood up and wiped his face on his shirt and let go. "You've got a nice yard for him? With shade?"

"Yes." I wanted to take Hank and run but I knew that would ruin everything.

"Your gram loves Hank." Noah wasn't expecting me to answer. He was just going over the facts. Convincing himself. He stared at the ground, all weedy dandelion stalks, blinking fast.

I hadn't expected Noah to cry, but that didn't stop me from feeling triumphant, too. I tightened my hold on Hank's collar and hugged him closer and thought about how Gram's house would be a little more the way it used to be, once she had Hank back.

Chapter 19

Hank and I were across the road and nearly to the canoe before Noah caught up with us.

He skidded to a halt beside us and, panting, announced, "I'm seventy-five pounds."

He'd donned his own ball cap (it said, WHAT HAPPENS AT SYCAMORE LAKE STAYS AT SYCAMORE LAKE) and wore an orange life jacket, the kind that went around his neck. A water bottle was clipped to a loop on his shorts and he held a pack of dog treats. They were a kind that gave Hank gas, just proving that maybe Noah wasn't as in tune with Hank as he claimed if hadn't figured that out.

Noah pointed to Hank and then himself. "Hank's maybe twenty-five pounds. I'm seventy-five pounds. What about you?"

"I have no idea. Why would I have any idea?"

He said, "Well, you're just a kid, too."

Pushing Eddie's camo ball cap back, I looked him over. All seventy-five pounds. Was this a trick? I wasn't good about figuring out tricks. I wasn't good at riddles, I wasn't good at test questions, and I guess I wasn't good at outsmarting a kid to get Hank back. "You can't have Hank back. You said. You said my gram needed him. No givebacks."

"It's not a giveback. I gave my word."

Noah then pointed at the canoe, as if that was supposed

to clear things up. "I'm just saying that having me come along won't make much difference. That maybe all together we're about the same weight as a grown-up. If we add it up."

"I know that." I didn't know that. I hadn't even thought of it. That Noah would want to hitch a ride in the canoe.

"Hank's a special dog," he went on. "You're going to need my help."

"I know all about Hank, okay?"

"What I *mean* is, me and Hank, we're simpatico." He thumped his chest when he said it.

I had no idea what *simpatico* meant, and I didn't ask. I snapped Hank into his life jacket. He wagged his tail so hard it almost hurt when it hit my leg, and I tightened my grip on the leash as Hank decided he wanted to sniff all along the shore. I bet the drained and swampy lake was a smell party for a dog. "I know all about how he doesn't go through doors," I said, winding the leash around my wrist.

Noah said, "He doesn't go through windows, either."

"Windows?"

Noah shrugged. "I was trying everything."

***

You might think a dog in a canoe was the problem, but Hank knew what he was doing. Hank wasn't the problem. Hank sat tall at the front, like our dog figurehead, and he was busy smelling all sorts of good things. It was as though he was sniffing his way home. Thinking of that made me happy and almost made me forgive the extra passenger. Did Hank smell Papa in the canoe? On his life jacket? Did he smell the water that was gone and all the fish, now suddenly closer to us? It smelled like a story. Papa, who liked to read about dogs and listen to people talk about dogs, said a dog can smell a layer of scent, like history. They can smell the order of things. They can smell how long a scent has been there, clinging to you or your clothes or on a tree, underneath a newer, stronger smell.

No, Hank wasn't the problem. The problem was Noah.

Noah sat in the middle, behind Hank, holding his leash. I sat in the same place as before. It all seemed like a good enough idea.

With the extra weight we sat low on the water, and I had to change up my stroke so I wouldn't hit Noah on the back of the head. Hank and Papa had been in the canoe a thousand times. Noah had obviously never been in a canoe before, or if he had been, it had been a quick trip that ended with a swim. He leaned from side to side to check things out, rocking us in the water. When he talked, he turned back to look at me. When he saw something or shooed at a cloud of gnats, he waved his arms as though he was the guy on the runway helping an airplane land. He couldn't get situated and wanted to cross and uncross his legs, except there was no room, so he couldn't change anything and had to stay pretzeled up. We may have weighed about as much as a grown-up, but we had six more legs than one. The only solution I had was to paddle faster, but already my arms ached and my hands were tired from gripping the paddle.

Almost right away, Noah told me about the rowboat.

I said how we didn't need a rowboat since we had a very

excellent canoe, and that a rowboat was more work and more to handle and a canoe was better in shallow water, and Noah said how a rowboat was bigger, as if I didn't know that. He said he'd even row it, as if I didn't know how to row a boat, which I do. I asked, "Do you think I'm stupid?"

"That's not what I meant at all," he said, twisting around to try to face me. "You're not stupid if you don't know how to do something. I just meant that if you didn't know how, I did. Or we could take turns."

"Well," I said, and I felt like Gram, all cranky. "I wasn't planning on an extra passenger, you know. It's a one-person canoe. One person. Plus one dog."

I thought about Noah trying to get Hank through a window. I tried to remember the windows at his house, but I hadn't paid any attention. It was an old house. The windows were probably big. Were they up high from the ground? Or did he mean a small basement window? Had there been basement windows?

I said, "That rowboat will sink."

"It won't."

"Then why is it abandoned? You don't abandon a perfectly good rowboat with two oars that won't sink. If there even are two oars."

Noah insisted it was in good shape. "There are totally two oars. It's like it's waiting there for us."

"Could you just hold still?"

"Okay. Still as a statue." He laughed. "Still as Mrs. Cryer in the boat parade."

I didn't really know Noah Pham at all, but I knew enough to think *Don't do it*, and just as I managed to speak—"Don't do it!"—he did it.

He rose to his knees and whipped one torchless arm up in the air with enough momentum to wobble us and send one side of the canoe sharply down, slapping the water and giving us an up close and personal look at the muck. The bag of gas-giving dog treats flew out. Noah didn't want to lose the dog treats, and he reached and reached over trying to grab the floating package, and Hank, startled, didn't want to lose the dog treats, either. Hank jumped to his feet, paws scrabbling on the canoe bottom, giving a surprised bark as the momentum rocked us and I leaned to the other side, trying to keep us from capsizing

"Grab Hank!" I hollered.

Noah hollered right back that he already had him, and then it was just the soft sounds of the water and weeds lapping at the side of the canoe as we rocked back into place. Noah and I sat silent while Hank snapped his teeth at a gnat swarm, as though he was a Hungry Hungry Hippo. I had that almost-fell-down-the-stairs feeling.

"That was a close one." Noah slumped, and my whole view was his sad spine. Hank's leash was wrapped so tightly around his wrist that his hand was changing color.

Noah was a lot smarter than I was because that's all he did—sit sad and slumped. He didn't say how obviously that was a real close call, and maybe how a rowboat would be more stable and there would be more room, and how wasn't this all about Hank and not about you, Lolo, and your papa's yellow canoe, and you're trying to get this dog home to get your grandmother to love again, and who knows what Hank could get sick with in that water. Giardia. That was what it was called. What usually gives dogs bathroom problems. We bobbed along in the water, the wind pushing us a little in the direction we wanted to go, red-winged blackbirds swooping by, and somewhere, far away, cars rumbling along on the rumble strips that lined the road in front of Noah's house. Hank nudged the wet bag of treats and Noah dried it with his shirt and inspected the seal before opening it and giving him a couple. Hank ate them loudly, all chomping, happy, slobbering chewing, which Papa always said was a dog thank-you. Noah didn't say anything about the rowboat so I didn't say anything about dog digestion and the treats I had in my backpack. Easing my grip on the paddle—which I'd held as tightly as Noah had held Hank's leash—I aimed it over the water.

"Okay," I said. "Where is it?"

Noah moved slowly this time and stayed squared up with the front of the canoe and pointed at the long, skinny tree-covered island not far from shore and past the Burger Bar but in the opposite direction of home. He held his arm straight like an arrow. He didn't need to say anything.

"You're kidding me," I breathed. "No way."

He was pointing right at Mosquito Island.

Pretend you're an astronaut and you're the first one to ever land on a new planet. What do you see?

—Noah

When I look out of my big helmet that's as big as beach ball, instead of seeing red burning gases of death, I see that I'm at a place like Earth but it's not Earth. It looks like Sycamore Lake. The water is up to the edge of the dam, and the dam is perfect and there never was anything wrong with it. The lake is busy with boats and people having fun but not so busy that the line at the Frozen Fish is too long.

At my house, my mom and dad are both there together and they don't have anything mean to say to each other at all, but they also aren't totally silent, either. My mom says if you don't have anything nice to say, don't say anything at all, which sometimes meant silences could go on for a real long while. But because this is an alternative universe my parents are having a regular conversation. We have a dog. It's a mutt. It's my foster dog but now here it's my real forever dog. Also, The Brain is there. He's not my favorite person but I'd feel bad just crossing off his existence. And maybe the same for my stepmom. Because we do mostly get along, and she's The Brain's mother and I don't think my mom could be The Brain's mom because the learning curve would just be too much for all of us. So maybe I'm not on another planet. Oh no. Maybe I made a mistake and got into the time machine and not the spaceship and this is one year into the future!

Chapter 20

Everything was different near the island.

The grasses and weeds in the water were thicker the closer we got and it became harder to paddle. Every weed and plant and root tried to grab the paddle and slow us down. Sometimes I had to yank so hard to free the paddle I uprooted the plants. Carp, the biggest fish in Sycamore Lake, swam by just inches below the canoe, and I worried about them as if they were surfacing whales. We pushed past garbage: an orange cooler, a sunken cowboy boot, concrete bricks, soda cans.

Mosquito Island is a skinny island. It would probably fit inside the school's gymnasium except for the trees. It's packed with trees. There are sycamores that lean out over the water, their bark gray and white. There are native honey locusts, which grow clusters of long, sharp thorns that are like sewing needles. There are short and skinny pawpaw trees with their big green leaves like fans.

It even smelled different—fresh and earthy, like the woods, like spring mud, and less like the stinky muck of the lake.

I canoed up as close as I could, which wasn't that close since the tree roots rose all around the island like the back of some sea creature, and tipped my head up to look at a sycamore that leaned so far over the water it appeared as though it could topple at any moment. I told Noah, "Don't touch anything. Keep your hands in the canoe."

"You sound like the operator of the Tilt-A-Whirl at the county fair."

"I mean it."

"No worries," he said, tilting his head up, too. Hank's nose was pointed down toward the shallow water, sniffing.

Papa said when he was a kid, his friends would swim or boat to Mosquito Island and try to camp out, but no one ever succeeded. He said there was no place to sleep that wasn't filled with poison sumac. He said what land there was, was pretty much a bog. If it wasn't a bog, it was tree roots. He said kids lost shoes and tents and flashlights in the mud. He said, if you were lucky, all you'd leave with was about one hundred mosquito bites.

I said to Noah, "Eddie says Silas says there's quicksand."

"Silas is all talk. I'm not worried about quicksand. I know all about quicksand. I watched an online video about what to do. If I fall in. All we have to do here is get the rowboat and then row away." Then he asked me the question I'd been dreading. "What are you going to do with the canoe?"

I squinted at the island. I knew what I had to do but I didn't want to tell Noah. It was like writing in my journal at summer school. I just didn't feel like making it official. So I said, "You get the stupid rowboat and I'll watch Hank, then you and Hank wait in the rowboat and I'll deal with the canoe."

Noah tapped on the canoe's edge, where it was thin pieces of reddish wood. It was cherry. Noah didn't know all the ways the canoe was special, and I didn't tell him.

The tangle of tree roots began just feet from the edge of the dam, and so we all got out of the canoe. I parked the canoe in the sloppy mud and sat on the dam while Hank stretched out on the grass above me. Noah took off his shoes. I asked him if he was sure that was a good idea, and he said he didn't want to ruin them, and I said, "But you'll ruin your feet."

He shrugged and tightened the straps on his life jacket and asked, "If it's so muddy, where's all the poison sumac and all?"

"It's on the trees! Poison ivy is a vine that's growing on all those trees and poison sumac is like a bush or a tree or something."

Noah got a serious look on his face and straightened his glasses. "Right now, getting the rowboat to safely transport Hank is the most important thing."

I couldn't really argue against that.

There were no summer places right here because of the island. Maybe because there wasn't a view or room for docks or boathouses. The grass was high and weedy and filled with clover and swarming with sweat bees. I hate sweat bees. You can't really slap at them and their sting is more like a bite, and it itches about the worst of anything, except for poison ivy.

The next thing I knew, Noah smacked me square on the forehead.

"Yow! What was that for?"

"Mosquito," he said. He shrugged. "Sorry?"

"Mosquito Island," I muttered. Rubbing at my forehead, I could already feel the bump from the bite. "Give me some notice next time."

"Consider yourself warned. Wow. You're already puffy." Then he slapped my arm. "Mosquitos really like you. Guess I picked the right person to bring to Mosquito Island."

"What do you mean by that?"

"I mean, if I stick close to you, they'll all bite you and not me."

Then maybe I saw a mosquito on his arm, so I slapped him back, even though he was right. I was the kind of human mosquitoes viewed (smelled?) as an extra-tasty snack. There were too many insects snacking on me in the grass, so I stood, waiting, slapping myself. Noah waved and headed out, crawling over the roots just like they were one of those spiderweb playgrounds.

I yelled, "It better have two oars!"

Noah just kept climbing over and through the roots with his bare feet as though he was climbing the ribs of some just-discovered Sycamore Lake monster. When he reached the island proper, he stopped to wave again and hopped up to point at a bare foot. I didn't know what he meant by that. Maybe to show me that he still had them. Then he disappeared into the shadows of the island and its thick tree cover.

I unfolded the doggy bowl and poured some water for Hank and then I slapped at mosquitoes and danced around the sweat bees, and after Hank had a drink I found a stick and we played fetch. Hank bounded after it and trotted back proudly with it between his teeth. "Aren't you a good boy?" I asked as he dropped it at my feet. "I've missed you so, so much. Nothing is the same without you." Hank nuzzled my hand

and I scratched his ears, and we played catch some more until we heard a creaking from near the island and then a splash. Hank stood at attention, tail up, and barked.

Noah had shoved the rowboat off the edge of the island and it slapped onto the water. "Two oars!" he shouted, right before he scrambled after it. There was a long, frayed rope that trailed behind the boat, and Noah trudged into the lake, lunging after it.

I cupped my hands around my mouth. "Do you need help?"

Noah yelled, "Nope!"

That's when Noah started screaming. "It's quicksand! It's quicksand!" He stumbled deeper into the water, and all around him the water turned black and murky as he kicked up everything at the bottom. Who knew what was down there. It was dark and soupy and yucky. That's what was down there.

Noah's eyes were hidden behind the mud-spattered lenses of his glasses. He slapped at the water. Hank ran up and down the edge of the dam, barking. I told Hank to stay. To Noah I yelled, "Just stand up!"

During a regular summer, the lake wasn't all that deep. Six or seven feet maybe. Which is plenty if you're a kid. It's over your head if you're a kid. I yanked off my sneakers and ran out to him. Sloshing toward him through the mud, tree roots catching at my feet and shins, I missed everything but mostly I missed six feet of water I could swim through. I waited for the quicksand to grab me and swallow me up the way it was swallowing Noah, but it was just thick mud. Sediment. There were meetings about it. Folks said the lake would have to be dredged and scraped all clean before it could be filled again.

"It's okay," I told Noah. I tried to use my I-know-what-I'm-doing dog voice. "You've got this."

He looked right at me then, panting. His eyes were wild, like a cornered dog's.

"Grab my hand."

He shook his head. "I'll pull you in, too. Then we'll both be stuck."

"Just grab it. Come on. We'll walk toward shore."

"I can't," he said. "What will happen to Hank if we're both stuck?"

I tried to grab him, anyway, but he was so freaked out he smacked me as he flailed. That's when I grabbed him. Just grabbed him like I don't know what. Like a person grabbing someone's life jacket and hauling. Like that. It was a fight but it wasn't, and if it was, I won. There was a great squelch of mud, as though the bottom of the lake were giving him up, and he stumbled forward onto his hands and knees in the shallower water at my feet. I almost believed it really had been quicksand with how loud that noise was.

I said, "It was just mud. Are you okay?"

He only nodded.

"Come on," I said. "I have snacks."

Chapter 21

Noah cleaned his glasses with dribbles of water from his bottle and then waved them around to dry them because he said he'd be in so much trouble if he scratched the lenses and his shirt was too dirty and it was wet, anyway. We ate on the root bridge between the island and the land while Hank snoozed on shore, his leash looped around the trunk of a skinny pawpaw tree. The root bridge wasn't exactly comfortable, but it was fun, and Noah said it was neat to think that no other person in the whole world had maybe ever sat here like this, and wouldn't I like to go back in time and fly in a time-travel drone and see what the world was like, way back in the past, to see who lived here, or to see the glaciers and the mastodons?

"I mean," he said, "would we even *recognize* it? We wouldn't even recognize it. It would just be a swamp."

I said how I wasn't a fan of time travel.

"But just to *look*," he said.

"Maybe," I agreed. "Just to look." I guess since it was never going to happen, it didn't matter if I agreed or not.

Then Noah said, "If anybody can invent a time-travel drone, it's my brother The Brain. He's my younger brother. Half brother. The half part is the brain part."

Noah told me how his brother was born premature and how he'd been a bit little hairy. "But it was cute hair. I don't know how to explain it. I wasn't expecting it, but I guess it's totally normal." He said, "He's not hairy now. He's just regular."

His brother's name is Brian but they call him Brain because he used to spell his name wrong, but also because he's smart. "That name thing notwithstanding."

"See," I said, "now that sounds like you're smart."

"That's a direct quote from my stepmom."

"So he's not ever going to go to summer school like us?"

Noah squinted up at the sky. He had the kind of lenses that automatically got darker in bright light, but I still wanted to warn him not to look directly at the sun. Maybe it was something not everybody knew, like how to sit in a canoe.

"I wouldn't say that. I mean, summer school is test practice and help and enrichment." He said *enrichment* the same way he said *notwithstanding*, as if he'd plucked it directly from a conversation with an adult. "A test is just one day. Like, it's just a few hours of your day on one day of your whole life. Everybody is more than a test. Everybody knows that."

"Noah. *Nobody* knows that."

He didn't have an answer for that. We had warm juice pouches and snack packs of cookies I'd swiped from Gram's cupboards. They were expired, just like her milk, but they still tasted good. Noah said how in his second-grade class, they did a unit on dinosaurs and used toothpicks to pick the chips out of the hard cookies and pretended they were unearthing dinosaur bones, and so now this kind of cookie always made him think about that and also owl pellets with mouse bones, because that was the next thing they picked apart.

He said how I shouldn't worry about the new baby because I was going to be just fine since I liked to take charge.

"Really?"

That made him laugh. Really laugh. Like maybe cookies could come out his nose. "Fetching Hank? Telling me what to do in the canoe? I mean, the lollipop thing? Come on."

"Wait. You don't really believe I took Silas's candy stash?"

Noah shrugged. "I don't know. When would you have done it? When did you eat all the lollipops? I just wanted to get it over with. Get out of there. I mean, Silas probably just forgot he ate them."

I said, "Mrs. Cryer couldn't pound salt in a rat hole."

"What?"

"It's something my papa used to say. When he was mad at someone. Or if someone wasn't very bright. Because, you know, it's not hard to pound salt into a hole. I mean, I guess I don't think it is."

"But she's a teacher. She had to get a degree for that."

"Look," I said, "maybe she's school smart, but that's about it."

"It was a mean thing for a teacher to do, make that kind of threat," he said. "But she's been okay, aside from that."

"Says you."

Noah reached down and flicked at something dark on his

shin. It stayed right there. "What is that?" he asked. "Is it a leaf? A worm?"

I sat bolt upright so fast I got dizzy. "Noah! Noah!"

"What?"

"You don't know what that is?"

"No?"

I grabbed the carboard from the empty cookie package and poked at what looked like a soft lump of mud on his leg, but of course it didn't move. "It's a leech. Ugh. I hate leeches."

He poked at it again. It still didn't move. It was never going to move. "You mean like a bloodsucker?"

"Yes."

"Ugh! Get it off!"

"You can leave it on. Let it drink all the blood it wants and it will fall off in about an hour. Of course, it releases, like, blood thinners into…"

Noah slowed down as though the leech were releasing brain thinners. He blinked slowly at me and blinked slowly at the leech and then pushed his glasses back up his sweaty nose. When he spoke, he spoke without moving. Without moving his jaw even. "Get it off."

"Okay." I paused. "Don't suppose you've ever watched a video about leech removal?"

"No."

I wasn't sure he was even still breathing.

"Do it," he said.

"Let me think."

I'd had leeches before. What had Gram done? She never got worked up about it. It was a muddy lake, so it wasn't that unusual, even if it put me off swimming for a few days.

I slurped up what was left of my juice ("What are you waiting for?" Noah said, still hardly moving, and somehow he still made it sound like a wail) and flattened the pouch, and told Noah to swing his leg around. He moved like some kind of frozen robot, as though the leech would attack his face if he moved too fast. I pulled on the skin of his dirty leg and slid the pouch right between the leech and the skin, fast as I could, and flicked that half-fed bloodsucker back into the water.

Noah was released from his frozen spell and said how, wow, I really knew what I was doing, how did I know what to do, it was way easier to get off than ticks, and don't worry, Hank was up-to-date with his shots, and this is the kind of stuff kids should learn in summer school, summer stuff.

"That's camp, maybe." I'd never been to summer camp and I probably never would, but I'd seen a lot of movies. "But it was my gram who taught me."

"Thanks," said Noah. "You're good at this stuff."

I didn't want to dampen his good mood, but I still told him, "Come on. We better check between our toes."

Imagine a fish started talking. What would it say?
—Noah

The fish popped its head out of the water and glubbed.

Me: *How's it going?*
Fish: *It's warm and shallow and there are some spots where I can't breathe.*
Me: *So don't go to those places.*
Fish: *But I'm a fish.*

It was a catfish. A bottom feeder. With whiskers. The catfish said the water was too shallow and too warm and it all just sat still, the water, which let plants grow, like algae. The regular kind and the toxic kind.

Fish: *The algae likes the phosphorus in the goose poop and the nitrates from the farm fertilizer that washes in, but I don't.*
Fish: *Do you know how much one goose can poop in a day?*
Fish: *Two pounds of poop a day.*
Me: *You're a fish. How do you know?*
Fish: *This is my life. Of course I know this stuff.*

Chapter 22

When the news got out that Sycamore Lake was going to be drained and there wasn't going to be a real Sycamore Lake summer and probably no tourists would show up and how we all had to go without it for a summer so the dam could be fixed, Mom and Dad talked a lot about the greater good. That meant while all this wasn't any fun and it wasn't good for the town or the businesses right now, it had to happen in order to save the lake and the town and probably even save lives.

That's what I thought about when Noah and I lifted Papa's beautiful yellow canoe over the gnarly tree roots and then when I carried it on my shoulder and hid it in pricker bushes on Mosquito Island and slid the paddle in underneath it.

Noah asked, "Are you okay?"

"Just hold on to Hank."

He didn't even roll his eyes. "Right."

I thought about the greater good in the rowboat, too, because it was ugly. There was nothing special about it. It was a dirty aluminum boat streaked with green paint. I couldn't tell if it used to be green or if someone had started painting it green and never finished, or if it was supposed to be some sort of homemade camouflage.

The oars were wooden and splintered. The rowboat had been turned upside-down in the mud of the island, so it didn't need to be bailed, but it was still filled with cobwebs and the kind of flat, dark bugs that liked to crawl around in hidden places.

It was awkward and heavy. It wasn't sleek or beautiful like the canoe. I rowed with every muscle I had. I braced my feet on the gritty bottom and pushed with my legs as I leaned back and pulled the oars to my chest. It was loud as the oars creaked and groaned.

But it *was* bigger. There was room for our backpacks and all our legs. I sat in the middle seat and Noah sat facing me with Hank between us. Even though the rowboat was ugly and awkward, we were both kind of proud that we'd managed it and that we'd coaxed Hank in and the only problems were about four hundred mosquito bites and one welt from a leech.

Still, I'd figured out a way to row that would help scratch the mosquito bites on my arms when I pulled back on the oars.

Noah took a turn rowing and I sat on the front bench closer to Hank, who stuck his head over the side of the boat almost the same as if it were a car window. Noah tried to go fast, as if he had something to prove just because I hadn't wanted to switch because all this was my job. Every now and then an oar slipped out of his grip and jerked the boat.

"Do you know what time it is?" I asked. "Do you have a watch?" We'd spent a lot of time at Mosquito Island. The sun seemed like late afternoon sun.

Noah grunted out his answer. "No. Don't you know what time it is?"

"No. That's why I asked." I couldn't tell if it was later than I thought or just getting cloudy. I squinted off to the west, but I couldn't really tell anything. Especially not the time.

"Didn't you bring a cell phone?" he asked.

"No," I said.

"Well, that's stupid."

"I didn't want to lose it. Or get it wet."

Noah said, "This is exactly the kind of situation you need a cell phone for."

"Did *you* bring a cell phone?"

"No," he said. "I was kind of in a hurry. You might remember?"

"We should switch back," I said. "I want to row."

"I got it," he said.

I was a better rower but I was tired and my arms hurt all over. Noah was faster but I thought it wouldn't make any difference because he pretty much rowed us in a zigzag and I had to keep pointing out the direction we needed to go.

Noah said he'd never rowed this long or this far, and I told him how in that case he wasn't doing too bad. He laughed. "Be pretty pathetic," he said, "if I lived on a lake and couldn't row a boat."

We didn't say much after that. Hank and I faced the front of the boat, sitting up at the tippy top where it made a V, as Noah jerked the boat across the water. How long had we been rowing? It seemed like hours, but it couldn't have been hours. Maybe just one or two. I wished it hadn't rained. If it hadn't rained, I would have started earlier and Hank and I would be at Gram's by now. A scattering of lights started coming on at the places where people lived year-round, but the dark and empty summer places around the lake stayed dark. The village was still off a ways, and even though we were on a boat traveling across water, I couldn't forget that everything was different.

Design a hamburger
—Noah

Don't gag or pretend to throw up, but my favorite kind of burger is a cheeseburger but a cheeseburger with blue cheese. The trick is not to look at it when you eat it because blue cheese is spotted with blue or green because it's moldy, but it tastes very good on a hamburger. The best place to get this burger is at the Burger Bar, which is on my side of the lake by the winery. Outside the Burger Bar it always smells like fish because it's on the canals and folks are always fishing there. Even though it smells like fish, you've got to eat outside. There's nothing like eating outside. I haven't had a blue cheese burger in over a year. My mom tried to make it but it wasn't the same. The other thing you can get at the Burger Bar is free drink refills. You'll hardly be down to the ice at the bottom of the cup and someone whisks it away for more. (They also have nice bathrooms, but they are FOR PAYING CUSTOMERS ONLY.) We watched the Fourth of July

Boat Parade from there last year. My mom says I have a good imagination (especially when it comes to ways to get a dog), but I never could have imagined then that the Human Statue of Liberty (you) would be my summer school teacher, that I'd be in summer school, that the lake would go all weedy and shallow, that no tourists would visit this summer, that the dams would all have to be rebuilt because they were old and not very good to begin with and people built houses too close to them, or that I'd be on local TV. Or that you'd be on local TV. When one of the city TV stations played some cell phone video of the boat parade to talk about the dam and the water levels, there you were, dressed in your gray robes, wearing your green Statue of Liberty headpiece, and holding your torch. Did you know I'm in the background? I'm the kid on the dock feeding french fries to the geese.

Chapter 23

Things were going okay until the fireworks.

Dogs hate fireworks.

Papa never went to any. The best place for dogs during a fireworks display is the basement (according to Papa), but because their house doesn't have one, Papa took any dogs to the back bedroom and changed the radio station from oldies to classical music and hung out with them. We hadn't had a Fourth of July with Hank yet. Maybe Gram or I would have would have just stayed with Hank in the living room.

But it wasn't the Fourth of July and it wasn't full dark when I might have been on alert. When I might have had a chance to grab tight to Hank's leash or shout to Noah for some help. Hank knew before Noah and I did, which is the way it is with dogs.

First there was a high whine, like a faint and faraway screech in the sky. Then a boom followed by crackles.

Noah jerked and nearly lost both oars, and then hissed, *"Fireworks,"* as though it was a very bad curse word.

But it was too late. Hank was gone. He'd yipped and scrambled over the edge as the leash whipped out of my grip, and then he splashed into the lake.

Noah yelled and stood up on the seat, making the whole boat wobble.

I hollered for Noah to sit down and row, and Noah hollered

for Hank. As if Hank were coming back. There was another whine, boom, and the water around us sparkled with green-and orange reflections. Birds darted past. Hank was swimming away. He was a spot in the distance.

The whites of Noah's eyes were practically glowing in the approaching darkness. He shucked off his shoes and threw off his ball cap, and next thing I knew, he'd jumped out of the boat, except he fell, catching the backs of his knees on the edge, and the boat flipped. I hit the water with an almighty splash. The water wasn't cold and it wasn't deep, but it was still a surprise. My knees banged the bottom and Noah looked like a swamp creature splashed with mud. For a moment, he was frozen. Was there really quicksand? Was he stuck? He took a few slow steps, the water up to his hips, and then he dove forward to swim through the weeds. He swam after Hank doing his own doggy paddle.

"Wait!"

Noah didn't even look back.

"I can't find my backpack!" Sticking out my arms and legs like an octopus I tried to find it. I grabbed at slimy weeds and I wondered if there were muskies in the lake—I didn't think there were—but they were big fish with teeth that sometimes jumped to catch a nearby land animal, and the mud was so thick and squishy I didn't think Noah had been wrong to worry about quicksand. I grabbed ahold of a strap and pulled my backpack behind me as my hot-pink dollar store sunglasses floated away.

Thanks to Noah's sideways rowing, we weren't so far from shore, or at least not as far as we could have been if we'd gone straight across the middle of the lake to get back.

The world turned tricky all around us. We stumbled up out of the water, squelching through the muck, not sure where the water ended and the shore began, at least not until we hit the weeds. They reached as high as our knees and scratched as we pushed through. I pulled my sorry, soggy, heavy backpack behind us and Noah raced ahead, scrambling up and over the rocky wall of the lake and up onto a green lawn. Somewhere out across the lake, another firework exploded.

Noah and Hank were somewhere up over the dam and on the shore by a big, old house that wasn't crowded by summer condos. I had no idea where Hank was, but Noah was running to a white gazebo between the shore and the house farther up the hill.

We weren't too far from the village, but all the same, we were at the worst possible place.

Back at Mrs. Cryer's.

Chapter 24

Her big white house glowed with light but I didn't see anyone outside, and I was glad. All I could think of was her standing on her dock, high above the water, in her floppy hat, and saying, *Isn't this just like you, Willow Weaver,* and I didn't know if this was just like me, but she was the last person I'd ever want to prove right.

"Hank? Here, Hank, come on, boy." Noah ran up Mrs. Cryer's lawn, calling out for Hank. I dumped my sodden backpack and went looking, too. How far were we from a road here? Where would Hank go? Would he find his way home to Gram's? I was sick and sad, but I also wondered what it would be like, if Hank sniffed his way to Gram's front door. I liked that. Hank barking. Gram looking out the window. Gram being so glad to see him. Right then, I wondered if Hank would solve this for himself, and he'd trot happily home, and I could say to Noah, *See? See how I was right? This is Gram's dog.*

Remembering what happened when I threw the plate and how Hank had busted out the door so fast he probably didn't even know he'd done it, I looked for places I wouldn't expect Hank to go. Like under the white gazebo that stood between Mrs. Cryer's house and the lake. There was lattice around the base with a small opening from a missing panel. Down on hands and knees I peered into the darkness and caught sight of a wet and muddy dog. "Hey, Noah." I called him over and pointed.

Noah huffed and stood with his hands on his hips, taking in the situation. We knew it wasn't good.

I told him, "I'll go look in the backpack. See what kind of shape the dog treats are in."

Water dripped down his legs. Shaking his head, he said, "We need hot dogs for this."

"I know that! But I don't have any."

"Maybe we could ask a neighbor."

"No way!" I tried to keep my voice down because I one hundred percent did not want Mrs. Cryer to come traipsing out of her house to see what was going on. *Isn't this just like you, Willow Weaver.* "Do you know where we are?"

"Does it even matter?"

"This is Mrs. Cryer's house. And she does not have any hot dogs. She is not a hot dog kind of person."

"I don't know, Lo. She's the Statue of Liberty. On a party barge. In a boat parade. I bet she has hot dogs."

"*Come on.* You know what she's like. She doesn't care about us, and she doesn't care about dogs, and we need to get Hank before she calls the police on us!"

Noah gave me a look, nudged up his glasses, and said way too reasonably, "I don't think she'd do that."

"Take off your stupid old life jacket," I told him. "You'll never dry off wearing it. And I don't want to find out if Mrs. Cryer would call the police. I know I'm right about her."

"Okay," he said, unbuckling his orange life vest. "But we're going to need hot dogs *and* a miracle."

Throwing up my hands in frustration, I said, "Standing around and talking isn't going to help. You said you had a special way with Hank. You said you got him to go through windows."

"I mean, it wasn't exactly like that."

I crouched to peer under the gazebo again. Mrs. Cryer's grass was green and cool and soft. Hank blinked at me and tucked his snout under his leg as he curled up and whimpered. Noah came up behind me, squelching like a swamp creature. Dropping to his knees next to me, Noah leaned forward and looked in.

Noah finally got to it. "Hank? It's all right, buddy. I'm here. I've got you."

Fireflies started to flicker around us. They seemed to rise up out of the grass, like they were the last bits of summer sunshine heading home. How late was it if the fireflies were out? Not afternoon anymore, that was for sure.

Cold, I took off my life jacket and wrapped my arms around myself. I could see the goose bumps on Noah's bare legs as they stuck out from under the gazebo. Now that the burst of fireworks was over and we were on shore, everything was quiet. Just crickets and Noah murmuring to Hank. It wasn't like any summer out on the lake I'd ever heard. No music, no flickering boat lights and hum of the motors, no voices carrying across the water.

I missed the hot feeling of the sun on my skin, the hot feeling of sitting in the canoe, and then how hot and sweaty I'd been in the rowboat. I could already tell I'd be sore tomorrow but now I was just cold. The sun was dipping away and my clothes were sopping wet.

We had to get out of here. Before Mrs. Cryer found us, and before we got hypothermia or something.

Noah crawled into the darkness under the gazebo. He spoke to Hank with that dog-love voice, that voice when all you had inside of you was love for your creature. "We can do it, Hank. We can do it."

Noah leaned into Hank and then Noah barked. Quiet. A standard kind of human woof. Hank didn't say anything in reply.

I peered in closer. I wanted to ask Noah all sorts of things, but the most important question—would it work?—would be answered one way or another, so I didn't say anything, just stayed crouched and peering inside, where it was hard to tell Noah and Hank apart.

Then there was a hot-dogless miracle.

Hank and Noah crawled out from under Mrs. Cryer's gazebo.

They were slow. Noah was on all fours and they leaned up right together and crawled shoulder to shoulder. The dog whined and the human woofed, as though he really had something to say and whatever it was he meant it. It was slow going. Gentle. Patient. Not the way it had been when Eddie had practically ridden Hank like a horse to get him in the back-yard. Once Noah and Hank were out, Hank gave a mighty shake, the kind that's funny but just gets anyone nearby wet, and Noah didn't come back up to his feet right away. He was still deep in the dog zone. Hank licked Noah's hands and then my stinky feet and I shooed him away because I didn't think lake-slimed sneakers were a healthy snack and took off his doggy life jacket.

"Wow, Noah," I said. "That's amazing."

Noah shook out his head and sat back on his heels and grinned. "I told you my methods were unconventional."

"Do you do that for every doorway?"

Noah said, "Sometimes. It doesn't always work, you know."

"Lolo! Lolo! Lolo Weaver! Lolo Willow Weaver!"

Mrs. Cryer had big classroom lungs, and she repeated things a lot, the way teachers do because nobody gets it the first time, except what she was repeating was my name and I got it.

"We've got to get out of here!" I grabbed Hank's muddy leash and tucked my head down. Eddie's camo ball cap was still on my head, except of course I'd been wearing it before when Mrs. Cryer had seen me in the canoe. "Let's go!"

But Mrs. Cryer was surprisingly fast and the three of us didn't escape in time. Maybe that was a teacher thing. Fast when they thought there was an emergency, except this time *she* was the emergency.

The first thing I saw were her painted toenails, a shimmery pink, and her fancy flip-flops. Beaded. I supposed there were a lot of things you never want to know about your teacher, like the color of their toenails, but mostly I was too surprised to see how she wasn't wearing sensible shoes.

Noah stood up and waved, and Hank tugged free of my hold on the leash as he went over to sniff Mrs. Cryer's bejeweled feet.

Mrs. Cryer was surprised to see Noah. Me, stranded, I guess she expected. "Noah Pham! Is that your rowboat out there, young man? What's going on?"

Noah explained how we'd capsized and Mrs. Cryer's eagle eyes zeroed right in on me. "What happened to your canoe, Lolo Weaver?"

I told her I traded it for a dog. "And him," I said, pointing to Noah.

She gestured to Hank. "And who's this?"

I stepped forward and picked up Hank's trailing leash even as Mrs. Cryer crouched to scratch behind Hank's ears. If I didn't have so much to hold against her, I might have been impressed that she was interested in my dirty and stinky and wet dog. "That's Hank," I said. "He's my grandmother's dog." I didn't look at Noah. "The fireworks scared him."

"Oh, of course they did!" She cooed at Hank's muddy face and scratched behind Hank's ears and said how smart and pretty he was and weren't those fireworks awful, just awful, how could people do something like that to a poor pooch? I guessed she was one of those dog lovers who only loved dogs and not people.

"Well, we better get going," I said, taking in how the darkening sky seemed to be about the same color as the lake and the overturned gray rowboat.

"But how?" Noah asked.

I waved my arm half toward the shore and half toward the lake, trying to look as though I knew what I was doing though of course I didn't, but Noah and Mrs. Cryer and maybe even Hank fell for it, because Hank didn't even bark or whine or sniffle as if he smelled the uncertainty in me.

I grabbed our life jackets and my dripping-wet backpack and started walking away. We could cut through yards until we came to some of the construction, and by then we'd be close to the school. Once we were at the school, we'd be practically in the town. Once we were in town, we wouldn't be far from Gram's house.

Turning, I waved to Mrs. Cryer. "Bye, Mrs. Cryer! Thanks for your help!" Some people you like saying goodbye to more than others, and Mrs. Cryer was one of them. Even if she'd been nice to Hank and even if Papa said you could tell most everything you needed to know about a person by how they treated a dog, it didn't matter because I already knew how she treated me.

Noah hurried after me, calling to Mrs. Cryer as he went. "Bye! See you!"

Mrs. Cryer gave a little wave and told us not to get in any more trouble and then turned to go back to her big house.

Chapter 25

Mrs. Cryer went her way and we went ours, walking across her lawn to a row of skinny juniper trees. They're the type of tree people put up to have a tree fence and these stood in a line like a bunch of green, bushy pine cones. I said, "That was really cool, what you did back there. You and Hank. Getting him out from under the gazebo. It was like a doorway, but worse because it was smaller."

"You think so?"

"For sure."

"Hank always looked so sad about it, you know? Not going through doorways and being left out. And I thought, it's hard to be a dog in a person's world. So one day I just got down next to him and wanted to speak his language, and, I don't know, it worked. It doesn't always work. But sometimes it works. He likes to know I'm trying to be real with him."

We stopped at the line of trees.

"What do we do now?" Noah asked. "What do we do without the rowboat?"

"Walk. It's not far." I still had my shoes on my feet, but they were heavy and soggy and rubbed, and I was getting blisters.

Noah said he was sorry.

I didn't like it, Noah saying sorry to me. "Blame the fireworks."

"Yeah. Stupid fireworks."

On land, there were even more smells for Hank. He sniffed around the trees. As long as he could smell things and pee on things and not encounter architectural features he was pretty happy.

I gave Noah the leash and slung on my backpack. It was cold and heavy, but I didn't see a better way to carry it.

Hank had found something interesting to sniff, and Noah didn't turn the leash back over to me but rather tugged Hank back. "Can't you make a phone call?" he asked. "Would your gram pick us up? I bet she's worried about you."

"She thinks I'm staying at Ivy's. Come on. Let's keep moving."

I'd only taken about two steps before Noah asked, "What about Mrs. Cryer? We should have asked to use her phone."

"No way." *Isn't this just like you, Willow Weaver.*

"We should have asked. That's all I'm saying. I'm pretty sure there's like a law or something. She has to help us. If we ask."

"It doesn't matter. She hates me. There's no law. That's stupid." I didn't want her help, anyway. "She'd only say how a lack of planning on my part doesn't constitute an emergency on her part. Because she's the kind of person who likes to say that."

"I've never heard her say that."

"But she would like to. I mean, she threatened not to let us go home."

Noah tugged Hank back from whatever smelled interesting in the junipers and nodded slowly, unsure. "Okay. You said it's not far?"

"Not far at all," I said, which I knew to be a one hundred percent out-and-out lie, but I was going to do this and I wasn't going to let Mrs. Cryer see my failure ever again.

I set out for the next landmark, which was a giant spruce tree in the next yard. It was as big around as a car and its branches swept out low over the ground.

Noah trudged on behind me as Hank pulled up ahead, tugging us toward the shore. Noah tried to pull him back but something had caught Hank's attention. It looked like rocks.

Right then, Noah cried out, disgusted, "Argh! Ugh! Cripes!"

"What?"

"Poop! That's what! Ugh! I stepped in some." He hopped around on his toes and rubbed his bare feet in the grass, hoping to clean it off.

"Goose poop," I whispered. It was a warning. "It's goose poop."

Noah said, "That's always going to be funny. I'm sorry you got in trouble for it though."

"Noah. Those are geese. Not rocks."

I was too late. Hank already knew. Hank hated doorways but he loved chasing geese. It was the kind of thing we learned fast and that Papa had only let happen once.

"Stop!" I shouted. "No, Hank!"

Happy and barking, Hank sprinted down toward the shore and roused the geese from their sleep. They honked and flapped. Some flew low to the water and some honked and ran right back toward us.

"Hank! Here!" I tried to say it the way Papa did, firm but not mean, my voice low. "Here! Here!" I shot Noah a glance in the dark. Would he chase after Hank on all fours? But all Noah was doing was hop-skipping after me, as if goose poop had the power to take away his ability to run.

Hank probably weighed more—I have no idea how much a goose weighs—but the geese were taller. With their snake-like necks extended and their beaks out and their big wings outstretched as though they were going to wrap us up in them, the geese were big, scary animals. Hank skittered, barked, dug in his heels, and then came running right back at us, chased by a goose.

And since Hank was booking it, he was gone in an instant, and that honking, mad goose was coming toward us.

I turned and ran.

Noah staggered behind.

"Come on!"

The goose looked like it was going to take a bite out of his knee. Dropping back, I grabbed Noah's hand and pulled. "No! Bad goose!" I thought about Eddie's rocks. How I hadn't known if I would ever really throw them, and how now I had my answer, because all I wanted to do was run away.

We made it back up to the line of juniper trees and then the big spruce, and I could already tell Hank was looking for trouble and he'd found something new. "Noah! Help me with the leash."

The goose was still making its way toward us, and I didn't even think or wonder if I'd been inspired by Noah and his barking. I acted like an attacking goose. I stuck my arms out big like I had my own set of wings and bobbed my head like I had a beak to bite with until the goose flapped and settled its wings in, turned, and waddled away, as though all of this was no big deal.

Noah still ran as though he was a puppy who'd never felt grass on his feet before. Maybe I needed a leash for him, too, for crying out loud. I didn't have time to get angry, though, because the wind kicked up and I could smell what held Hank's attention.

"Oh no."

Even Noah sniffed, sticking his nose up, as if he needed to be sure. Because it's the kind of smell that threatened something so horrible, you just had to be sure, even if there was no mistaking it.

"Get the dog."

But it was too late.

Write your own test question
—Noah

A skunk is
A. a harbinger of doom
B. a nocturnal mammal
C. hard to smell ahead of time if it's downwind
D. all of the above

Chapter 26

Skunk spray is bigger than stink.

You can taste it. You can feel it in your mouth. It chokes you. It is horrible. It burns your eyes and your nose, and you feel as though you might never get a good lungful of air ever again, it will never taste or smell clean and fresh again, nothing will ever taste or smell clean and fresh again. Everything would always be this stink. Hank tried to run away, but he just ran in a circle, barking, and came back to us. Noah and I dropped right to the ground and pushed our faces into the grass. As if that would help. Maybe it did. Who could tell?

Hank whined and Noah coughed and gasped.

I tried not to breathe but that never works, and the grass tickled my face and I couldn't stand it but I didn't dare lift my head.

Noah wheezed, "You're crying."

"You're crying, too."

Noah gasped, "It's the smell. It's in my eyes."

Breathing was bad enough, but talking was worse. It let that skunk stank go deep inside me and I wondered if it would wither my organs. It changed the whole world. All the smells, the air, the mission of getting Hank back to Gram's, everything I thought I could do burned and stunk.

This was all my fault.

"This is all your fault," Noah said.

"Me? You had Hank!" I shouted it still facedown, right into the grass. I hoped my face wasn't in goose poop. "You had the leash!"

"You had the leash in the boat!"

"You let go so he could chase the geese!"

"Don't get mad at me!" *Cough.* "This is your thing!" *Cough.* "I wanted to get help!"

"Well, Mrs. Cryer's not going to help us now!" I almost felt good about that part. No way would Mrs. Cryer let us touch her phone, never mind allow us in her car for a ride home. "And you invited yourself, in case you forgot." My voice was hardly a voice. I tried to talk and hold my breath at the same time. I kept my eyes squeezed shut, but that didn't help, either. "You just got into my canoe. And then you made me leave it on Mosquito Island."

"You were stealing my dog!"

"Hank's not your dog! You said! You said!" I coughed and coughed and coughed. My eyes watered. The stink was everywhere. It was everything. There was no wind or breeze, and it hung in the air as though it was there to stay. Forever.

Noah didn't say anything and Hank whimpered and I was surprised they didn't run away. Hank. Or Noah. Maybe the spray weighed us down. How far could skunk spray spread? Maybe we'd never escape it, but for sure it had to be the worst right there and right on the three of us. I peeked at Noah. He was curled up on his hands and knees, like a rock, or the lump of a goose. "There's a gas station not too far from the school," I said. "If we need tomato sauce to get the smell off. But maybe, like, we'd get free ketchup packets?"

Noah sat upright and held his hands over his face. "It's too many ketchup packets. It would never work."

"Okay. Let's just get going to my gram's."

Noah shivered and threw his arm around Hank.

"Are you cold?"

"Not really."

"Noah, we can get to Gram's. We've got this. She can give you a ride home." I skipped how she didn't like to drive at night. "Or we could just move out of the stink zone. We're as close to home as we've been all day."

"It's okay, Lolo. I'm good here. For a minute. I mean, maybe we'll . . . air out. And skunk spray can travel for miles. I bet it's all over the lake. I bet you can smell it at my house. There's no escape. Resting a little won't make a difference." He lay down on the grass and curled around Hank and Hank curled around him. I stayed right where I was. Sitting up straight. Noah petted Hank's wet fur. I petted Hank, too. He was such a good dog. He was the best dog.

"You're a good boy, Hank," Noah said into the dog's wet, stinking fur. "You were awesome, getting out from under that gazebo." Somebody sighed, and I didn't know if it was Noah or Hank. "I sure am going to miss you."

He said, "It'll be good for that grandma to have somebody to love again, right?"

He said, "Don't ever forget how much I love you, okay?"

Then they both looked right at me and Noah said, "I'll be ready to go in a minute."

I said how there wasn't any hurry.

I didn't know if that was true. It was getting later and later. Darkness wasn't going to make anything any better. When would Gram expect me home from Ivy's? How long would Ivy wait before sending out a search party?

Hank snuffled and curled up next to Noah. Right before Hank settled down he swung his head toward me and gave me a long look. Like he knew something. I scooted a little farther away and lay back and looked up the sky. It was quiet. After a while, there was a soft sort of sniffle and I hoped it wasn't a skunk sound. Did a skunk clear out after it sprayed? Or did it hang around and enjoy its power?

I rubbed my burning eyes and tried holding my nose closed, but all that did was fill my mouth with skunk taste. I peered over at Noah.

"Hey, Noah?" No answer. "Noah, are you awake?" He'd fallen asleep like an exhausted puppy. "Noah?" I poked his bony back but he didn't move.

I took Hank's leash and slid Noah's arm through it. Even in the dark, I could tell Noah's arm was bumpy with big bites and rashes. I wrapped the leash around his arm a couple times and hooked it over his fingers. Noah didn't move. He'd conked right out. He was out like a light. Hank was asleep, too, and didn't stir when I petted him. Hank's fur was matted and had turned dark with dirt. He stunk so much I couldn't even smell him anymore because I think my nose had stopped working.

Noah's hair stuck every which way. His shoes were gone. His glasses lay crookedly across his face. They were wrecked up on a lawn above the broken earthen dam of the gone lake, like a shipwreck, a kid and his dog, asleep.

I didn't know how he could sleep, all skunked up and on the skunky grass with his nose in a wet dog's fur, but he did, and right then I knew two things for sure. Noah loved Hank. He loved Hank more than I said Gram did and more than even I did. That's why he was willing to let me take Hank. Because he loved Hank and because he thought I was right about it being best for Hank, even though Noah knew he and Hank were simpatico. I still didn't know what that word meant, but I think Noah meant they were two peas in a pod, because that's what they looked like just then, Hank and Noah, curled together.

The second thing I knew was I was being selfish, not brave. Trying to get Hank away from his new home, even if Gram needed him, needed something, and maybe what she needed wasn't an answer I could find for her. And now look at us, stinky and dunked.

I patted Hank's wet fur and told him, "That was real good how you got out from under the gazebo. I'm really proud of you. Papa would have been so impressed."

I told Hank, "Noah really gets you."

I told Hank, "I don't know what I'm going to do about Gram."

I told Hank, "Never forget how much we all love you. Me. Never forget how much I love you. But you and Noah belong together. He's your person, Hank." I wasn't sure, but it's possible Hank peeked at me, sleepily, with one lazy eye.

For just a little bit I felt good. I'd made the right decision. I knew it as sure as I'd ever known anything.

And then I realized a third, awful thing.

"Noah! Noah! Noah!" I grabbed both his shoulders and shook.

"What? What's going on?"

"Noah! Can you move? Are you paralyzed? Move your arm!"

Noah sat and pushed up his glasses and said, "I guess I'm beat. Sorry. Why are you freaking out? What's wrong?"

But I'd moved on to Hank, tugging on his leash harder than I should, trying to get him to stand, to move, to do anything. He stood and then plopped back down onto his haunches and yawned.

"He's tired," Noah said. "It's been a long day. The *longest* day."

I grabbed a fist of Noah's wet and muddy shirt and said, "The water. The *water*, Noah. The algae."

"Blue-green," Noah whispered, shooting to his feet, stumbling. "Toxic blue-green algae. But does the lake have it? Are there warnings?"

"Maybe! By the beach in town, but it's not even a beach. But it can happen even just if it's a warm day. And there are so many geese right here, it's going to be all pooped up! And rain! It rained this morning. Doesn't rain do something? It washes all the farm fertilizer into the water!" Hank was standing now and sniffing the grass, and I held on tight to the leash. I didn't tell Noah about the lake that had toxic algae and no one was allowed to swim in it for years, and sometimes the animals that drank the water—like pet dogs and deer—were found dead at the shore.

"*Lolo*. Why didn't we realize sooner? We should have realized sooner. Right when Mrs. Cryer was here. Before the skunk. What are the signs?"

"I don't know! I don't remember! Death!"

"What?"

"There's one kind that can kill a dog." I took a deep breath like the ones in my mom's prenatal yoga videos and tried to calm down. It didn't work. "But, um, I think if it were that kind—the brain one, the neurotoxin—he'd be dead already."

"But the other kind? Does he have it?"

"Maybe. He could." We both got on our knees and looked up close at Hank, who didn't even shy away from us, but if there was anything to tell we didn't know it. "I just think you're supposed to get your dog to a vet right away. I think that's the rule. Even without symptoms."

"Like what? Throwing up? Falling over?"

"Yeah," I said. "All of that."

Now I could tell Noah was crying for real.

"You and Hank stay here," I ordered. "I'm going to go get help."

"I guess it's good you're going to be with Hank," Noah told me. "You and your gram. I didn't even know this stuff. I don't even know how to take care of him."

I was already running and yelled back to him, "Noah, are you bananas? Didn't you hear anything I said while you were sleeping?"

A smell you remember
*   —Noah*

Skunk spray is like smoke
And you are the lousy meat
You are stink bacon

Chapter 27

Now that the fireworks had stopped, the lake was dark and quiet and lonely, all except for Mrs. Cryer's house. Her house was lit up with golden light shining out the windows.

Because it was an emergency and because Mrs. Cryer already didn't like me, I wasn't shy. I ran up her front steps and pounded on the door and leaned on the doorbell. "Mrs. Cryer! Mrs. Cryer!"

The lace curtain on the window next to the door flicked open. So I pounded on the window. "Mrs. Cryer!"

I figured Mrs. Cryer would be relieved not to hide what she felt for me when she opened her front door and shooed me off her porch and out onto her lawn and breathed in the great stinky skunk smell of me, and she'd know that she was really, truly right about me all along, as though that stink were the truth of me, finally revealed.

When she opened the door she gasped in horror, though maybe she was just trying to breathe. I had to admit, I had some sympathy for her for that. And she shooed me away, but I only went down a few steps.

"What's going on?"

"It's Noah and Hank," I answered. "Hank's been poisoned by the lake water. We've got to get him to the emergency vet's office. It's out by the highway, you know, by the warehouses—"

Mrs. Cryer held up a hand to stop me and stared right into my eyes. I didn't know what she was thinking. I didn't want to know. I was ready to beg or tell her everything was true—she could call me whatever she wanted and I'd never say different about eating every last one of the stollen lollipops and I was just a big baby about journal writing.

"You've got to help us," I said. "You've got to get Hank and Noah to the vet. Please. And please drive fast."

"But what about you? Don't you have to get home, too?" She looked at me as though I were a page of illegible kid handwriting and shook her head. "Oh, isn't this just like you, Lolo Weaver."

I didn't want to listen to her and so I pushed on. "You'll need to get Noah's parents because you have to pay up front at that place. And I'm warning you. Everybody smells really bad. And please, *please* don't be impatient with Hank. He's got issues. He can't hurry, okay? He's not going to hop right into the car. Even though it's an emergency. Even though it's the only way to save him—"

Mrs. Cryer grabbed my grubby arm before I could make a break for it and said, "Isn't this just like you, always thinking you've got to solve the world's problems."

"Mrs. Cryer?" I didn't want to cry. All of a sudden, I was so close to crying. What if she wouldn't help us? What had she meant when she'd shaken her head? Did she mean *no*? Hank would *die*. "Noah—"

"Oh no, Lolo," she said, and I thought how I knew, I knew

it, only Mrs. Cryer could be this mean. But Mrs. Cryer, still holding my arm, said, "I don't know why you think you're not coming with us. Do you really think I'm letting you loose alone in the dark?"

***

A lot of things happened quickly. We rinsed Hank with Mrs. Cryer's hose (her place was fancy enough that her hose had cold *and* hot water), and Noah tried coaxing Hank into the back seat but then finally wrapped him in an old blanket Mrs. Cryer had offered from her trunk and then Noah scooped Hank up and lifted him in. Hank didn't even fuss. That's when I got really scared. Even if Hank and Noah were Hank and Noah, that still didn't mean Hank liked doorways, and a car door still counted. So what was happening now? Before it had been only something serious to worry about, because Hank didn't have symptoms. We needed to get him to a vet fast, sure, but maybe he wasn't sick, not that we could tell. But now that he was so still it made me worry. Was Hank sick now?

Noah held Hank wrapped in the blanket. I sat next to them. Mrs. Cryer flipped on the high beams, rolled down the windows, stepped on the gas, and threw her phone into the back seat. "Call Noah's parents, the vet place, and your parents."

As the car zoomed through the dark, Noah put his face right into Hank's ear and woofed soft, like he had something to say. Hank didn't say anything back, and I felt like howling, just as I had the night of Papa's funeral. Except this time I did. It was just a soft sound. Just a quiet *arrrr-oooo*, a private howl that I'd had inside me for months. Noah woofed again, but if Hank had anything to say to either of us, we didn't hear it, not over the sound of Mrs. Cryer's fast car on the country road, not over all the horn honking at Noah's house and then when she pulled in to the vet's parking lot, crooked and with brakes squealing, and leaned on the horn. A burly vet tech came out and whisked Hank away, and if Hank had anything to say right then it was too late.

Chapter 28

They made us wait in the fenced exercise yard. There were no dogs in the dog yard, just me and Noah, filthy and foul, all quiet, waiting. We didn't have anything to say. It was hard enough to worry and hope and breathe all at the same time.

It wasn't long before Noah's mom caught up with us and arrived in the parking lot. After a while another car pulled in. Mrs. Cryer's car was still there, and the other cars had to park crooked around it. Only one person got out of that other car, and he didn't have a pet. Noah groaned and dropped his head to his knees. "My dad," he said. "He's not a dog person."

As we waited, I thought about a lot of things. One of them was that time travel journal topic. But not time travel, exactly, but how we were already and always traveling in time. It didn't matter, time was always going forward, even if you didn't think it should and even if everything in your heart was about *now* or *before*.

"It's been so long," I said, even though I didn't know how long we'd been there. Not in any precise way. It all felt like *too long*.

"That's a good sign, isn't it? Hank's going to be okay. Right?" Noah sounded hopeful and like he was desperate for me to agree. "He has to be okay. He's here. He's still here, and the vet is helping him."

"I don't know." We had spent a long time in the hospital waiting room for Papa, and then when we got news it was the worst kind.

Noah didn't say anything more, and we just kept on sitting in the dark.

When the door to the exercise yard finally swung open, Noah and I scrambled up to our feet and Noah grabbed my hand and squeezed and I squeezed back.

The veterinarian, Dr. Fabbro, had a lot she wanted to explain—liver toxins, neurotoxins, charcoal (which she'd fed Hank), intravenous fluids (which Hank was getting), observation periods (overnight), prognosis (very optimistic), fast thinking (getting Hank here), and situational awareness (shallow and stagnant water was always going to be a problem). All we cared about was seeing Hank, but she said we had to come back in the morning, she was sorry, but she didn't want to agitate Hank, and "Well…" she said, still standing far back from us.

"We stink," I said.

"Yes," she said.

"We're also very dirty," I said.

"Yes." She looked at Noah's bare feet. "And shoes *are* required. But it's okay. It was an emergency. I'll have our tech unlock the gate and you can meet your parents in the parking lot."

Noah asked, "Hank's really going to be okay?"

"I believe so. But we still need to keep an eye on him."

She sighed. "I see it more and more as our waterways get warmer. Sycamore Lake is so shallow and stagnant and warm right now that it's just so easy for the toxins to grow. They're mostly caused from runoff and fertilizer, and here, believe it or not, one of the culprits is all the goose poop. Even if it sounds funny. It always gets me. How it rhymes."

"Oh no," I said. "It doesn't really rhyme."

"Of course is does. It's not a true rhyme, all squared up, but it's a different kind of rhyme called an imperfect rhyme, or a slant rhyme, where the vowel sounds rhyme."

We stared at her, and she shrugged. "Sorry. My husband teaches poetry."

"Like," Noah started, "for kids older than us?"

"Oh yes," she said, "for college students."

Noah said I should tell Mrs. Cryer about how goose poop really was a kind of rhyme, but I said it felt rude, after all she'd done for us, and Noah said how Mrs. Cryer was a teacher and teachers always say everybody should always be learning. I said maybe I'd write about it in my journal, and Noah said, "Oh, man, I've got a *lot* to write about now."

Mrs. Cryer gave me and Noah rides home because she said her car was already skunked-up. Before, when we were scared about Hank, it hadn't been weird. Being in Mrs. Cryer's back seat. Now we noticed how her car was nice, with soft seats. She dropped Noah off first and then we made our way around the lake and into the village, going the opposite direction to the evacuation route arrows and where all the signs said VACANCY or CLOSED. I told her she could just drop me off at Frozen Fish, thanks.

She said, "I don't think so, Lolo Weaver."

"It's close. It's right there." Practically. Pretty much. "Please," I said.

Mrs. Cryer crept the car forward until she was across the street from Gram's house. On the other side of us was the dark hole of the lake.

"If you turn and go down the alley I can go in the backyard. I can't go in the front door. It goes right into her living room."

Mrs. Cryer sighed, aggrieved, and turned into the alley. She'd barely stopped the car before I had the door open and my feet on the ground, ready to run.

"Hold on," she ordered. Some habits are hard to break and listening to a teacher is one of them. Even though all I wanted to do was sprint the last bit to Gram's, I slowed and looked back, and if what she said next stopped me altogether, even if just for a second, well, I'm not telling, and Mrs. Cryer probably has student-teacher confidentiality or something like that.

"I know you didn't take that candy!"

Time machine 2
—Noah

Is it okay if I rewrite this one, Mrs. Cryer? Because if I had a time machine I would have never let go of Hank's leash. I'd have held on to it the whole time in the rowboat instead of rowing and he'd never have jumped out of the boat when the fireworks went off. If I couldn't do that, I'd never let him chase after the geese, and because I was going back in time, I'd know that there were geese sleeping on the shore, and I'd also know where tthe was a skunk hiding, and I'd skip the skunk. I'd know where all the poison ivy and poison sumac is on Mosquito Island or in Mrs. Cryer's yard, so I wouldn't be so itchy and blistered.

I'd also go back and never feed a goose anything, not even a Burger Bar french fry, not anything.

But even if I couldn't change anything, I'd still go and I'd still do it all over again, because now Hank is my forever dog.

Chapter 29

Turned out, scrubbing your grandchild like a dog in the yard was an act of love. Gram told me.

I'd forgotten how strong she was. She about scrubbed my skin off, about scrubbed me bald.

I whimpered like a dog in a flea bath.

Gram just kept on scrubbing, like it was exercise, like I was a tarnished pan, like I'd be a hairless wonder when all this was over.

Between gasps, because sometimes she tried to hold her breath when she leaned in, though we were so close what good would it do, she said, "You're old enough to do this yourself," and "What a stinking mess," and "Good grief, Lolo," and the classic "What were you thinking?" Once in a while she laughed a little, though it always turned into a wheeze. "Scrubbed a lot of dogs, you know. At least I don't have to tie your leash to the tree."

It was as though all the scrubbing powered her up.

The way to get rid of skunk spray is to wash everything with a mixture of hydrogen peroxide, baking soda, and dish soap. Don't mix the ingredients up ahead of time. Gram started in on me right away because she said it's best to do it sooner rather than later. I stood dead center in the middle of the yard, waiting for her to mix the solution together because she didn't want me close to the house, and wondered if the neighbors could smell me. Was it the same as when the skunk stink blew through the neighborhood and everyone ran to close windows? Did I smell as bad as an actual skunk? I wondered if anyone at Noah's house knew the recipe for de-stinking.

"Keep your eyes closed," Gram warned me.

As Gram scrubbed, I felt like a soda can getting shaken up. I was filling up with something, and it was different than that flash of anger that I felt after Papa's funeral or when I claimed I'd eaten all the lollipops.

Once in school we watched a video about bees. To get the bees out of the hive, the beekeeper smoked them out. The beekeeper waved her smoker around and the bees started flying out into the cloud of smoke. The film said how the smoke was to distract the bees and get them to leave the hive, so the beekeeper could inspect it. I felt as though I was full of bees, waiting all this time, and now they were buzzing until they just couldn't be inside me anymore.

"Gram?"

She was scrubbing my legs hard enough to make me wobble on my feet and activating every bug bite on her way, but she stopped right away when she saw I was crying and grabbed me into a soapy hug.

"I'm filled with bees."

She pulled back to look at me, maybe thinking my brain lost oxygen due to skunk spray. "Lo? What are you talking about?"

"The baby," I told her. "I'm worried about Chickpea Garbanzo."

"Nothing's wrong with the baby. The baby is as snug as a bug in a rug and right where the baby is supposed to be. That baby and your mom are doing just fine. And your mom is where she needs to be, too."

"But I'm scared." All the buzzing filled me up.

"I know, honey, I know. It's not an easy thing. But it's going to be all right."

I wanted to take her words and believe them, but those bees made me say, "But it might not be. It might not be all right. Like with Papa. It wasn't all right with Papa."

"Well," she said, her breath a little shuddery. "Okay. Ah, jeez, kid. I don't know what to say. This is hard for grown-ups, too. For me. But I think it's going to be fine. Your mom is going to be fine and that little pumpkin is going to be just fine."

There was more. More buzzing.

"I messed everything up. I'm always messing everything up. I'm going to mess up being a big sister, too." I put my wet head on her shoulder.

"Lo," Gram said, "you're a fighter. And your heart is just so big. I don't know how that's messing anything up." She wrapped her arms around me and squeezed me the way Mom did, like she was a sea creature and I was the snack. Then she said, "You better go on and run to the shower."

While I scrubbed again in the shower, Gram washed my clothes with laundry detergent and baking soda and then hung them out on the line to dry, even though the sun wasn't up yet. We left them there to air out for about a week. They were still

there, dry and stiff, when I headed back to summer school on
Monday.

Describe a time when you were kind
—Noah

*Mrs. Cryer, I think maybe you should keep a journal and
write with us because you were kind when you gave me and
Lolo and one sick dog a ride to the vet in your car. I'm sorry
about your back seat but I liked the way you drove, with
the pedal to the metal and as if all the yellow lights meant
hurry up and get through instead of slow down. It's not like
there's any traffic around here anymore, anyway. This morning when I took my seat, Silas turned around and gave me a
look that wasn't kind and I said, "What?" which wasn't very
kind, either, and he shrugged and turned back around and
Max said, "Who smells like wet dog?" I said how it wasn't
me, because I had brand-new sneakers and they smelled like
new sneakers. I didn't say that my old ones were at the bottom of Sycamore Lake. Max also asked if I had the plague,
because why did my arms look like that, and I told him it
was poison oak or poison sumac or poison ivy.*

Max: *It's poison something, that's for sure.*
Madison: *I have a scar. See? See that scar on my arm?*
Poison oak last summer.

Eddie: *I had it all over my legs once. I sure tanned funny that summer.*

Cameron: *Where did you get poison oak?*

Me: *Mosquito Island.*

Max: *Oh, man.*

Cameron: *Nobody's supposed to go to Mosquito Island.*

Silas: *What? You've been to Mosquito Island?*

Me: *Lolo went, too, and she doesn't even have a mark on her.*

(Which was mostly true. A few bug bites don't count. You can get bug bites in your living room.)

Silas: *Lolo? For real?*

Max: *No way!*

Madison: *Lolo can do anything.*

Ivy: *You bet.*

Eddie: *You know it.*

Everybody turned to look at Lolo, but Lolo was looking for her desk. It wasn't hidden, it was just back in the middle of the room with everybody else's. She had new shoes, too, and a row of mosquito bites across her forehead. That was nice of you to move her desk, Mrs. Cryer. Also when you opened the window.

Write your own test question 2
—Lolo Weaver

A human baby is
A. *a small mammal*
B. *a nocturnal animal*
C. *a stinky mammal*
D. *all of the above*

Chapter 30

Chickpea Garbanzo did, in fact, remind me of a bean, but a kidney bean, the way she was curled and the way she was a little red yet. She was so tiny and fresh I laughed. Dad had me sit in the special hospital room rocking chair and put a pillow on my lap and then he settled her into my arms. She was wrapped tightly in a lightweight white blanket with pink-and-blue stripes and had a tiny hat on her head. Her head was about as big as my fist. She looked like a caterpillar. Noah was right. Human babies are strange creatures. I stuck my finger beneath the blanket and peeked at her shoulders, and sure enough, she was a little fuzzy. She blinked up at me like a big-eyed bird in a nest. "Hey," I told her. "We've got this."

Mom and Dad said her name was Summer, but we all called her Bean for a long time.

It had taken me a little while to get up to the hospital room to meet her because Gram drove slowly and took the back way and circled a long time until she found a parking spot she liked, far away from anything and under a tree, and then when we got to the sleek, automatic doors of the hospital I did a Hank.

The door went *whoosh* open and *whoosh* closed when folks walked in. It opened and closed like it was a gate to a whole new world—one where problems were fixed, or one filled with new problems. Or as if they were the doors on a time machine, maybe.

The last time Gram walked out those hospital doors she no longer had Papa. When Mom went through the hospital doors after the doctor told her to go straight to the hospital (Dad said he pushed her in a wheelchair) she thought everything in her body was growing a baby just the way it was supposed to and she was just fine.

Gram grabbed and squeezed my hand. I knew from the scrubbing just how tough she was. How her hands were wrinkled and spotted like Papa's. She complained about the spots and rubbed lotion into them every night. I thought I should tell her how they were strong hands that did a lot of good things. I squeezed back, but I still didn't go through the doors. People flowed around us. They didn't have any problem going into a time machine or they didn't even know. I wanted to warn them—*Be careful! It's all going to be different! There's no going back!*

Whoosh. Whoosh.

The cool air-conditioning blew out toward us on the hot pavement.

Gram said, "There's no hurry. There's a little walking trail around a pond if you want to take a break."

"Are there geese?"

"Probably."

"Maybe not," I said.

She might have cracked a smile. "Sure thing."

As more people went around us, Gram pulled me off to the side, near one of those giant concrete balls between the edge of the parking lot and the sidewalk. It felt cool and rough.

Finally, I said, "That baby will never know Papa. A whole new person in the family who'll never know him."

"I know that. Believe me, I know that."

I sliced my hand down like a karate chop. "Boom," I said. "Like the door's closed forever, and now we're in a whole new room."

"I hear you," Gram answered, slowly nodding and digging into her purse for a tissue and pressing it to her eyes.

I said, "It seems more real that Papa is gone, maybe."

"I suppose maybe I've thought the same thing."

"You have?"

"Sure. A little bit. I wish I had some philosophy or wise words for you, but all I can say is that's how things work, isn't it? And what are you going to do? Hold it against an itty-bitty baby? I sure hope not. That doesn't sound like you, Lolo. Your grandfather would be tickled pink to have a new grandbaby. Okay? Now come on, let's go see that little Chickpea."

***

Dad took me back to Mosquito Island to get the canoe. We drove over and then Dad suited up in his waders and I wore Mom's and walked over, avoiding any possible quicksand. When I dragged the canoe out of the bushes, Dad ran his hand down over his face and did that real big sigh I get a lot. "Criminy, kid." Then he got distracted by the mosquitoes and said, "Let's get out of here," and we walked it back to shore. Dad took some pictures of me to send to Mom with the canoe hoisted on my shoulder and surrounded by roots and pawpaw trees. "You're lucky your mom is too pooped to get worked up about this." He also said a lot of stuff like, "Holy moly," "Jeez Louise, kid," and "You promise this isn't where you met the skunk?"

"You mean an island skunk, Dad?"

"I wouldn't put anything past those creatures."

We loaded the canoe into the bed of his pickup and then laid on the horn when we drove past Noah's and then Mrs. Cryer's even though I told Dad that wasn't her style.

It seemed as though the rebuilding of the dam took forever with road closures and the loud construction noise, but by the next spring the lake was allowed to fill to its normal levels, and we were back to a Sycamore Lake kind of summer. Swimming and boating were all allowed again, and the tourists came back and finally (mostly) overtook the goose population. Some buildings that had been built too close to the dam had to be torn down, and even though it was the right thing to do, some people were really upset about it. The docks, with new rules about placement, got put back in, and the Frozen Fish opened up again. One of the souvenir stores and a diner stayed closed. Wetlands were created to help filter the water and reduce the chemicals from the runoff that got into the lake, and in the late spring part of the lake was dredged. Tons of dirt was pulled out and given to local farmers to put on fields. The mayor said how some of the best farming soil in the state was at the bottom of our lake. There were still toxic-algae warnings, and we always checked at the beach or online before we went swimming. Dad stayed on with two jobs all through the spring until the water was back, and while that made both him and Mom exhausted, he earned enough money to buy their first place to rent. Gram helped a lot.

The Fourth of July Boat Parade is going to be back, too, and Mrs. Cryer is going to be the Statue of Liberty again. I'm going to wave to her when the line of boats goes past our new spot on the lake if my parents haven't rented it out that weekend. Mrs. Cryer really came through when Noah and Hank and I needed her, and I might not say this out loud because people don't like being compared to dogs, but it's true: Just the way a dog's a dog with dog issues that you'll never figure out because a dog won't explain them all to you, it can be like that with a person. There's always going to be something about a person you might not ever figure out and understand, and it doesn't matter. You just have to know that's who they are, all the good and all the bad. So I'm going to be sure not to miss that part of the boat parade, not even if Gram needs my help.

Because I like to help Gram with Roscoe. Roscoe's an old and creaky basset hound (mostly) with a droopy old face and droopy old ears and a droopy belly that drags on the ground when he walks, but Gram says he's her kind of dog: slow, old, and tired. She said all that in a doggy-love voice, which was actually the same voice she used for the baby, but if you're from my family nobody thinks that's weird. Old foster dogs are harder to place because people are looking for puppies, and old dogs are less exciting and likely have health problems, but Gram says their hearts are good for loving all the same. Roscoe and Hank aren't exactly best dog friends—sometimes we meet up at the dog park on Noah's side of the lake—and Roscoe's more of a snoozer, but if anybody can get Roscoe to play it's Hank. Hank's not perfect on doors and he'll probably never be. Noah said he gets them about sixty-five percent of the time, and I told him maybe Hank needed to go to summer school. It was funny, but maybe you had to be there.

Acknowledgments:

After my first book was published in February 2020, the country went into lockdown, and yet *Itch* still found readers. From my end it seemed like magic, though of course it wasn't. It was the work of readers, booksellers, book lovers, teachers, librarians. Thank you!

Special thanks to everyone at Holiday House, including Theresa M. Borzumato-Greenberg, Sara DiSalvo, Darby Guinn, Laura Kincaid, Erin Mathis, Michelle Montague, and Shelia Hennessey (at PRH sales). Thank you to Nicole Gureli and Kerry Martin, who both took such loving care with the beautiful jacket and book design.

Deepest thanks to my wonderful agent, Alyssa Eisner Henkin, and my fabulous editor, Elizabeth Law, who helped me discover Lolo's story during some hard pandemic days.

Thanks to my parents and our own single-person, lightweight pack canoe for some wonderful summer days in the Adirondacks. Who knew what could come from paddling through the water lilies?

Thank you to my home team for your support, insight, enthusiasm, bird identification skills (sandhill cranes!), school-supply lending, and hole-punching assistance.

And finally, I'm grateful to you, dear reader, for shar Lolo's story. I think this quote from the educator (and member of the Reading Hall of Fame) David Harris Russell says it perfectly: "A writer only begins a book, it is the reader who completes it."